Assassinated by Love
By S Courtney

The Illusive Lovers Series
In
A Secret And Lies Production

Copyright

S Courtney

Contents

NOTE:

This story contains: Language, graphic violence, sex, dom/sub situations, pet play, age gap, and constant use of the word "daddy," if any of this bothers you, this may not be the book for you.

S Courtney

Colin

I thought lying and hiding behind a persona was best to keep me alive. In a world full of wolves preying on vulnerable sheep, I was a hunter, constantly moving and keeping anything I do on a need-to-know basis to protect me. I do the dirty work so my clients can keep their hands clean.

Who are my clients?

I know as much about them as you know about me and what I do. I know that the criminal world will contact us to get rid of their competition and enemies with no trace back to them. What was once taboo to hire contract killers became a much-needed relationship among the bottom feeders.

So, it's easy to figure out, I'm an assassin. The twist is we are hired by criminals but run by a small task force of the government to take them all down. We kill two birds with one stone.

I've done some pretty fucked up things in my career, I've sliced a man's tongue out of his head, I've pulled the trigger hundreds of times to end the lives of those who feast on the weak and take advantage of the desperate, and I never once second-guessed any of my assignments, except the last one.

And it's all because of her.

One night, after wiping out an entire crime organization including their notorious mob boss, his underboss, counselor, and five captains, I was waiting on my next assignment when I received a message to hang out with my best friend Vincent.

Vincent: Hurry up! I have a sexy one for you and I need you to distract her from her friend so I can hit that!

Me: Whatever, I'm almost there.

I arrived at Flaherty's Irish Bar & Grill to apparently entertain the friend. I round the corner to see an anatomically enhanced bleach blonde on Vincent's lap. I don't know how old she was, but her surgically altered face said she was much older than she was portraying.

Her body said I attend college and my sugar daddy paid for my tits, but her face said she was about to celebrate her 30-year high school reunion.

Her much younger friend was seated next to them, downing her drink as quickly as possible while she was being forced to watch them molest each other to bad rock music. I wonder if the MILF was trying to compete with her. Definitely not a fight she would win. I exhale and walk towards them when he spots me.

"Finally, what the fuck took you so long? Hey, this is Kandi and Sunny. Ladies, this is my buddy, Colin."

I'm thankful he wasn't too drunk and let my government name slip. I look at him and nod appreciatively.

Sunny, the woman on his lap, licks her lips and winks at me before shoving her tongue down Vincent's throat. His hands roam her body, then he smacks her ass, causing her to squeal before reconnecting their lips, muffling her giggling.

Why am I a witness to this? I hope she wasn't fantasizing about some threesome/orgy-type situation. I need a drink, no, I need a double shot of Jameson Black Barrel.

Vincent is one of two people outside the agency who know who I really am and what I do; even my family doesn't know, for their safety. The only other person is my princess, the light in my cold, dark world.

And that was only out of desperation...desperation to keep her. I had to prove to her that she was worth putting it all on the line and that I trusted her. But I was really worried if she could handle my truth?

And now to how I met my princess:

Vincent and I were hanging out one night at his place. I was on standby for my next assignment and happened to be close enough to hop a plane home. It was nice to do something normal.

Vincent opens up his laptop, "Dude, I seriously need to get laid. It's been like five days, I'm so pent up." He's hurting after five days? I'm holding a record here. Usually, after a kill, we get what we call a killer's high, and our senses become extra sensitive and highly responsive. Sex can be beyond incredible if you ride that wave. But with no prospects, I usually hit the gym.

I hear him tapping away on his keyboard as if he was answering an email or messaging someone; judging by his previous statement, it was probably the latter.

I chuckled, "Looking for an escort service you can afford?" I shake my empty bottle at him. "You want another beer while I'm up?"

"Yeah, I think there's two left. And no, smartass, I'm going on one of the many sites I'm a member of. This one's a sugar daddy site where I meet hot, young girls to fuck. Legal aged girls!" He quickly adds before I could raise my brow.

I reach down for the last two beers before grabbing the pretzels on top of the fridge.

"A what?! Isn't the main goal to finance their lavish lifestyles, not fuck them?"

He takes the last swig of his current beer and shakes his head while popping the top off the fresh one, "No, you choose the type of sugar baby you're looking for. They got prudes, but they also have girls who'll fulfill every wet dream you've ever had. You can personalize what type of sexual relationship you're looking for, too."

He types in the website address and a pink and white banner pops up with all types of sweet treat gifs...good grief, are those sprinkles falling from the sky?

"Sweetsugar.com?"

He rubbed his hands and licked his lips like a dirty, old man. "Yeah, buddy, the best thing to ever happen to a lifetime bachelor like me. I spend a little money here, pay a bill or two, and in return, I get a marathon sex session. Plus, they're all young, supple, and nubile. It's way better than beating your meat to a paper woman."

Vincent is only a year younger than me, but he is a proud member of the permanent bachelor society. He's been that way since I met him.

4

I, on the other hand, had a different path. I spent men college years and part of my twenties like everyone else, bouncing from relationship to relationship trying to find the one. Along the way, I learned about what I like and don't like. I realized I like calling the shots and being the lead. I took one of those quizzes that said I was a dominant type personality.

I wanted to know more, but then I got recruited and I didn't have time to pursue anything. Having to be so secretive was not ideal anyway. I was forced to become content in the bachelor life like Vincent until I wasn't, which happened a couple of years before I hit the big 4-0. I guess this was my version of a mid-life crisis.

I peer over his shoulder, watching him log on to see a grid filled with young women's pictures and some of them are borderline pornographic that pop up.

Well, it's one way to get someone's attention.

He clicks on his notification tab to see he had a couple dozen likes, messages, and a few voice recordings. I can only imagine what those audios held, but I'm guessing it was probably something like a clip from Pornhub.

"See, I can pick and choose who I want to finance and fuck. I don't even have to limit myself to just one…and I don't." He chuckles as he scrolls past the many blondes, brunettes, and even a few redheads.

"You're a perv, man."

"Don't judge what you haven't tried. Besides, you are in no position to hold a relationship so why not have a bit of fun and release some tension in the meantime? They don't need to know who you are. They can get to know Colin, not," I hold up my hand to cut him off, even hearing it makes me feel a way. He nods understandingly and continues, "When you retire is when you can settle down and all that. Here…" He logs out and angles the laptop toward me. "Make an account," I raise my brow at him, and he rolls his eyes, "Look, I'm not expecting you to screw the first pair of tits thrown your way. Just look around; you never know what could happen."

I give in, sighing loudly to indicate my reluctance. I lean forward because he has such a small laptop.

"Sweet sugar, don't resist temptation. Enjoy our sweet treats. Oh, brother…"

I started filling out the sign-up page.

"Username…hmmm…"

"I know! How about assassinating that ass?!" He almost falls off the arm of the couch, laughing.

Is he serious? He can't be serious.

"Absolutely not. What about killer instinct?" I type it in, and it says the username was already in use, but I really like it. It suits me.

"Killer instinct…69." I know, cliche. I hit enter again and it goes through.

"Nice, now fill out your personal stats."

It asks for the usual, you know, height, weight, age, etc. I don't mean to brag, but I think I still look great for my age. I'm a gym rat and I try to stick to my diet, shopping at local stores, and farmer's markets.

I'm a towering 6 foot 4 with blue-gray eyes and brown hair. I typically wore it short on the sides and the top a little long and swept back. I usually sport a beard, at the most, or the least a goatee with side stubble. I have not seen myself clean-shaven since I could grow facial hair.

I consider myself classically handsome, a gentleman who could wear a suit and make panties drop at the sight of me adjusting my cufflinks and then giving them my prize-winning smile while standing there with my hand in my pocket, James Bond style.

This is not to sound arrogant or cocky, but to keep the confidence within me. At my age is when it all starts going downhill with even the smallest amount of doubt. After spending some time describing myself, it asks what type of girl I'm looking for. Honestly, I don't even know.

"Hmm, age range 18 to 30," I wondered if you're 30 would you still be considered a sugar baby? I guess so depending on how old he is. The sugar daddies range up into their 70's.

I continue, "hair, no preference, weight, no preference, eyes, no preference. Highest level of education? Hmm, minimum high school, college is a plus."

"I don't know man, the dumber they are, the better…." Vincent singsongs while texting on his phone.

"You truly are an embarrassment to men. Let's see, monogamous? Absolutely. Polyamorous? Not a chance." I hear Vincent groan and slap his hand against his forehead. I don't share what's mine, plain and simple. I ignore him, "sexual or non-sexual relationship? Sexual." He hoots and claps his hands, scoring a victory for sin.

"Okay, now I click the attributes I want from this list, right?" I clicked several and the last question pertained to distance; I chose within the U.S.

"You don't want to trim that down a bit? That's a large area."

7

"I can pick up and leave whenever I'm not on the job. I don't want to limit myself yet. Besides, this is your stupid idea and if it goes bad, I am going to put you at the top of my hit list." He laughs as if I'm joking.

I hit enter and get confirmation that I joined a sugar daddy site...what have I gotten myself into? The agency is going to love this new bit of information. I immediately logged off and handed him his computer to shop around for his victim of the night.

"Let's see if Nariah or Teri are online to chat and then some. Stay if you want, but it could get X-rated really quick."

I held my hand up, shuffling quickly towards the exit. "No, thank you, besides, I'm exhausted. Enjoy."

I got back to my hotel room and ended up looking at my dominant quiz results that I have saved. I end up on a fetish site and signing up as well. There I can research the things that interest me and connect with those who have similar interests.

If I had to choose between the sites, I'd definitely drop the sugar daddy site, but I know Vince will check up on me and rag on me and call me a quitter. I'll keep it for now. Speaking of the site, curiosity got the best of me. I have no idea why; I'm probably no one's type. Once I logged in, I had two likes and no messages. I click on the likes to see two young-looking girls. One was a short, pixie-cut platinum blonde whose byline was 'If you aren't rich, then scroll by. My daddy needs to spoil me on command. I want it all.'

Deleted and moving on to the next, a tiny Hispanic girl with the most vibrant emerald green eyes I've ever seen. I scan her profile and don't see anything too scandalous, so I like her back.

I add a few pictures to up the ante. I also added them to the Naughtyfet site. I stand to stretch, rubbing my washboard stomach, before stripping down and hopping in the shower. My sore muscles screamed for it, my execution high had worn off without any vigorous activity and I felt it. I need to increase my cardio. I've got to keep up with the younger agents but don't be fooled; they don't call me Zeus for nothing. I am the upper echelon of mercenaries, there is nobody above me.

Fifteen minutes under the rain forest showerhead and I had finally relaxed. My mind wanders to my imaginary dream girl. Her features change all the time. There's something attractive about every woman, so to have a go-to type isn't possible for me.

Tonight, she had those piercing green eyes like that girl from the site, except she had flawless mahogany skin and naturally wavy hair that hit her shoulders. She wore nothing but a radiant smile as she took my hand and led me to bed, slipping under the covers and begging me with her eyes to follow. The velvety smooth cream color silk slides over my body, but it's her hands that heat me up quickly. I was rock hard before she laid a finger on me, but now she was stroking me slowly and methodically. She moaned my name in my ear but not my alias, hearing her call for the real me sent me into a frenzy.

I placed my hand against the shower wall as my other hand mimicked her movements in my fantasy. Up and down until she slid her body against mine and down until she was on her knees submissively. Her soft lips wrapped around me and I groaned to the change in sensation. They worked me over as my hands lock into her curls to guide her. She slid her lips up to the tip, sucking on me like a popsicle melting in the summer heat before she straddled my waist, lowering herself down as she gripped my sides, her nails dug aggressively into my skin.

My real-time movement sped up until I almost lost my balance in the stall while I imagined her riding me like her fucking life depended on it. When her orgasm squeezed me so heavenly, I couldn't hold back. I grunt as my release washes down the drain. I had to open my eyes because explaining how I injured myself while jacking off in the shower is not something I want to do. Vincent would never let me live it down.

Just like the time he got rug burn on his ass from a high-intensity one-night stand who reversed cowgirled him on the living room floor and I had to treat his burn where he couldn't reach. It was brutal and ironically shaped like a misshapen heart. I laughed for weeks especially after he banned that move from his sexual rotation.

I almost gave him an opportunity to turn the tables. After avoiding a potential sex disaster, I loosely wrap the soft hotel towel right under my Adonis belt. I trim my beard a little, then drop the towel before crawling into bed.

At 4 am my phone rang with another task. This time in, "Leeward, Wyoming? Where the hell is that?" I checked the bounty price and immediately packed my bag. Most jobs were little to no notice and with the constant movement, I didn't have much to pack. My flight was at 6 am.

I slept on the flight and drove two hours west of Cheyenne to a lodge in the middle of nowhere, wondering what type of evil could be dwelling in the back forests of Wyoming. I expect my dossier to be delivered by text soon. Still tired, I decided to lay across the bed to try to catch a few more Z's.

Just as my eyes comfortably closed, my computer dinged loudly. Groaning, I sat up and reluctantly opened it. I see two icons I don't recognize. I click the ice cream cone and it immediately goes to my still logged-in page on Sweetsugar. I have 88 new friend requests, 47-page notifications, 58 likes, and 27 messages.

Holy shit, I hadn't even put up a recent photo. My profile picture was when I was around 36, I wasn't as toned as I am now. I was in a three-piece suit for a wedding my sister begged me to attend. She was trying to set me up to settle down, but I ended up bedding the maid of honor instead. I introduced her to Colin, he was cold and calculated compared to who I really was. She told me she was only looking for no strings attached sex, so I gave her seven orgasms that night until the morning. Good times.

Anyway, I decided to wade through my inbox until I get the details on this hit.

I click the first message:

Hey daddy, you're looking good to me. Hit me up if you're ready to spoil me rotten; I can be a brat when I don't get everything I know I deserve.

Hit me back,
Bratzdoll19

I don't do brats and I can't see myself dealing with a temper tantrum every time she doesn't get her way.
Next.

Your cute, want 2 bang me? hit me on WhatsApp @...

Okay, didn't I state a normal level of intelligence, that definitely includes grammar. *You're, you're, you're...*I delete it as my brain mourns the cells I lost deciphering that message, moving along.

Hi daddy, I could use a good spanking from your strong hands. My name is Celeste and if you're ever in the Chicago area and want to meet up, let me know. I attached some NSFW pics for you to think about me. Hope to hear from you soon. XOXO,
Bbygrl312

Holy fuck!
These are not safe for anywhere, even in the privacy of my hotel room! They're all nudes and she had a pretty nice body, natural double D's, blonde hair, and dreamy blue eyes. Wait, is she wet in this pic? I zoomed in like a complete creep to confirm that indeed she was. Despite her forwardness, I sent her a heart to show interest.

I have to admit, I liked being called Daddy. I found a forum on Naughtyfet and introduced myself as a daddy-in-training looking for guidance. I made my profile public and copy-pasted from the other site except here my interests were dom/sub, submissive partner, and DDlg. My dominant side doesn't get too many opportunities to play, but I know that I'm interested in learning more about being a dom and eventually gaining a sub.

For these types of relationships, my princess would have to be special. It takes a high level of comfort to be in a commitment like that, it's give and take. She's putting a lot of trust in you to want to submit and allow you to take control.

You can't take that lightly; you can do a lot of harm but done correctly you are their caregiver and protector. I like the idea of caring and doting on her, showing her how much her daddy loves her, but I'm nowhere near that type of relationship yet.

An hour later, I deleted most notifications on Sweetsugar because they didn't meet my standards, or by accessing our database, I found… discrepancies. I ended up with five potentials and responded or sent them a reply.

Then my phone rang, throwing me right back into assassin mode, "Go for Zeus."

"Your target is Benny Princeton; his cattle farm is a front to the pallets of grade A Colombian ecstasy and crystal meth he ships throughout the countryside along the old cattle trails and mountain passages. The amount that has saturated the entire west coast has been astonishing, especially in Washington, Nevada, Southern California, and Northern Mexico. He calls his brand "With love" and has a signature logo on the packaging. That logo has been recovered at dozens of overdose cases, crime scenes, and rave parties. It's a pure product, making it more dangerous to those who can't recognize the difference and take lethal amounts. His product is responsible for over 50 deaths and counting; the youngest victim was 16 years old. We need to get him and his product off the streets."

I hear that number echo in my brain, *16, 16, 16.* When I was 16, I was trying to get the balls to ask out Serenity Howard, captain of the debate team, and my science partner, to the fall harvest dance. I dealt with depression and being picked on, but nothing that would make me turn to illegal substances, but times are different. The victim had their whole life ahead of them and now it's gone because of Benny.

"Who ordered the hit? Is this job clean or dirty?"

"The DeLano family, it looks like talks fell through between Benny and Tommy DeLano to mark out the territories in the west. Let's keep it clean, we need to find his distributors as well as Tommy's, we have a few leads, but if they hear about his gruesome death, they may flee the country and you know how hard it is to track them once they've gone international."

"Roger, I will do my best."

I hung up and decided to make the hit later tonight. I read my manifesto detailing Benny's dark history, using kids as drug mules on the entire west coast and even into Mexico. He didn't care what happened to them because they disappeared after they completed their job, and in this business, you know what that meant. He had countless victims due to the trafficking alone, not including those who succumbed to his substances.

His ranch was on an isolated parcel of land in the middle of nowhere. He probably thought no one would come looking for him and if they did, they'd be spotted a mile away on his security cameras that surrounded his property. But like most technology, it can be manipulated, and I had that ability due to the many talented agents in our division.

At 10:20 pm, I connect with my agent, who is currently hacking into the security system, so everything goes black when I give the word.

I park my car a quarter mile away and set it up to look broken-down on the side of the road, complete with throwing dirt on it to make it look like it's been sitting there a while. It doesn't look like much traffic comes back this way but just in case.

According to the satellite images, there's a back trail that leads to the perimeter of the farmhouse. Benny's one of those criminals who think living in the middle of nowhere hides you from everyone, but in reality, it isolates you and prolongs you from getting help. He'll be long dead by the time anyone is notified.

The trail leads to a path, which I believe might be a secondary escape route; it's slightly worn, indicating minimum usage. I keep my head on a swivel to avoid sneak attacks.

I observe one guy standing near a door that leads into the house. I hit the button on my earpiece. "Zeus to Socrates, ready to confirm the security cam outage." I hear the tapping of his keyboard, "Socrates to Zeus, clear to proceed. Remember that this is a clean job."

"Copy." I click the button to end communication.

Now that I know the footage is on a loop instead of live, I check my surroundings; the one guy, dressed in a black turtleneck and slacks, was still outside smoking. That doesn't scream security or bodyguard in the middle of Wyoming. He goes inside, but I notice the door didn't click. He can't be this irresponsible or was it a trap? My senses are on high alert. There is a chance Benny knew there was a hit out and was luring me in to kill me first. I needed to find another way in.

I snuck through the thicket of woods to stay hidden as I look for another entrance, finding a cellar-style basement door on the opposite side of the house.

Next to the massive doors were two tiny horizontal windows, one on each side. I peered through to see if anyone was down there but saw no movement and barely any light. I noticed the outside door is locked with a rusty padlock, an easier pick than anticipated.

I opened the creaky door, slip in, and close it back to avoid being spotted. It's pitch black so I slip on my night vision glasses and once activated I recognize I'm standing in the middle of his operation. Tables full of loose product and some packaged into bricks for easy transport. Before I take another step, I pull out one of my twin 1911 Nighthawk Chairmans with gold titanium nitride barrels and secure the suppressor.

A startling discovery when I turned to my right to scan the entire area and saw 10-15 women and children looking at me in complete fear. Too shocked to scream but I did hear a few whimpers from the younger girls, clutching onto their mothers for dear life. I could see they were wondering if I was there to hurt them or help them. What has he been doing to them? I didn't want to even think about it.

I bring my finger to my lips, whispering, "Shhh, I'm not going to hurt you, stay here, I will rescue you after."

I saw a young girl, about 10 years old, just nod her head, her mom pulling her closer, kissing her forehead. They look dirty and emaciated which fuels my anger further. No surprise he lured women and children; because the mothers are willing to do anything while trying to make a better life for their kids. What a fucking scumbag, I will make this quick, but it won't be clean.

I hear heavy footsteps above me and wait for them to dissipate before I approach the door leading into the main part of the house. I open it to reveal the kitchen. The dishwasher cycling into the next step in the washing rotation catches me off guard. Luckily my instinct and reflexes are keen enough not to fire wildly and give myself away.

I hear laughter and clinking sounds in the direction of what I think is the dining room.

"I see, umm, s-see your 50 and raise you 100, yeah." The male voice sounds weak and forced.

"You're bluffing! You're a goddamn horrible liar, but I'll gladly take your money and your dignity. I see your 150 and call. What d'ya got, kid?"

My target Benny is puffing on his cigar as he leans forward, waiting for his associate to play his hand.

The guy places his cards down gently, "I got two, uh two pairs, Aces and 8's."

Benny guffaws boisterously with the cigar in his mouth, his lackeys follow suit. He laid his cards down with flair, "Full house. You lose, don't forget the watch."

The guy hesitates before slipping off the gold watch that used to occupy his wrist. "But it was my grandfather's." But Benny swiped it anyway and chucked it carelessly into his pile of winnings.

"Well, it's mine now, don't bet what you're not willing to lose. Aye! Did any of you morons feed the workers?" They all shake their heads while looking at each other to see if someone did. I'm flabbergasted, especially by how late it was.

"Well! Dead workers don't make product and we got that big shipment going to L.A. in two days. Go fucking feed them!"

A tall blonde guy makes his way in my direction, heading toward the kitchen. I'm hidden behind a pillar, so as he walks, I shift my position.

"While you're down there, pick out a nice one for me for tonight."

That ignited my rage as I reached in and grabbed my second gun and suppressor. I also text the code: Rescue 10-15w/c. (10-15 women & children) 20 minutes.

I'm ready to deal out the pain, especially hearing Benny talk about taking one of the women up to his room. Not tonight.

If this job were dirty, I'd tie him splayed open and pour frying oil on his lap, watching him thrash around in pain, but the job was to be quick and easy. I'd be using my signature rounds that open into nine separate projectiles after firing. They take out whatever they come into contact with, rupturing everything. They're called eviscerators.

I wait for the blonde to return; he goes down into the basement with a tray of food and a bag full of water bottles. Luckily, he comes back with no one in tow.

Benny looks at him, "They're all eating; I'll grab the brunette with the yellow ribbon and her daughter." A twisted smile crept up on Benny's face as approval.

That was the girl who nodded at me. I distinctly remember that ribbon was in her mother's hair and the girl was just a child.

Just a child.

I didn't even stick to my plan as I roared from my hiding spot, firing on the two big guys by the front door entrance, hitting both targets in the chest. Their blood and other pieces of them splattered over everything in the immediate area as their body cavities were ripped open.

Benny's reaction was to grab the guy he was playing cards with and use him as a human shield. The kid's face filled with nothing but fear, doubting a lot of his decisions at this moment.

"I knew DeLano would try to take me out, that coward! If you want to kill me, you have to kill my son, too!"

Well, that wasn't in the dossier.

I didn't know he had a son. That threw off my concentration long enough for his alleged son to raise his gun and fired a shot that rang past my ear and hit the nearest solid object behind me, but I didn't see where the projectile hit. I could tell he never shot a gun before because he flinched when the shot fired. I think that and his poor aim caused the bullet to fly past me.

Realizing his mistake, Benny screams at him to fire again, but I already sent a round into his right knee. It exploded and his son went down. Next to him was the rest of his leg that was still standing.

That coward didn't even hesitate to run instead of tending to his son. He zig-zagged sloppily around, trying to avoid the bullets I hadn't even fired yet. His son's ear-piercing screams were ringing throughout the house while he tried to flee from me.

I was in the mood to humor him, following him around the house as he threw any and everything in my path. He finally found an exit and his movements quickened while mine stopped.

He reached for the handle, turned it, but he never made it past the threshold. I used a single round that pierced the back of his head.

They'll have to use his fingerprints for identification.

"DAAAAAD!!!!" I heard his son scream; looking over and realizing he had a front-row seat of his dad's violent death.

Didn't matter anyway.

I switched the magazine to regular rounds and put his 'son' out of his misery. I would need to confirm their relationship because there may be other family members to take out and eliminate the chance of a resurgence.

I slipped out the front door and back to the car. I had to duck behind when emergency services drove by with their sirens wailing. I checked my time, and it was exactly 20 minutes from the time I sent the text.

I was riding my killer high as I made my way back to the hotel. I found a few interesting daddy dom conversations going on in Naughtyfet and bookmarked them. Then I ended up with a very vocal blonde who was available for a quick sex chat. She wailed my name and I had to focus on my strokes instead of her screams to make myself climax. She sent herself to ecstasy and asked to do it again sometime.

I blocked her. She and her shrill moaning almost ruined my high. Never again. I closed my eyes and imagined my dream girl but this time she left me empty, both sexually drained and mentally alone, it was a double-edged sword.

How could I ever be exclusive? No woman would tolerate this type of relationship. My job ships me all over the continent, so I don't have a permanent residence. I live the hotel life; it just makes sense. Everything is in Colin's name except the offshore bank account, but Colin is my beneficiary, so I have access to my money either way.

My alias is Colin Wentworth, few know me as Daniel Denning. I use Colin for everything, so nothing I do professionally can be traced back when I retire and revert to using my government name. It's safer that way. I've been in my profession for almost 20 years and have seen associates come and go. The mystery of what happens to the ones that live after retiring intrigues me. One day, they're there; the next, we're meeting our new, younger teammate. I'm interested because I'm next.

At 42 years old and never married, it just doesn't sit right with me, but this isn't the job you could come home and discuss. Maybe these websites were what I needed as jumping-off points. What's the worst that could happen?

Colin

Eight Months Later:

Message from Theresa (brattybitch4u)

Who is Notyourdaddy19? And why did she like all your pictures? Are you cheating on me?!

Killerinstinct69: Watch your mouth. I can't stop people from liking my pictures. How can I be cheating? We aren't even together.

Brattybitch4u: I'll yell and scream all I want! I want her blocked immediately! I'm your only girl and I don't share! Either block her or lose me, what's it going to be?

Killerinstinct69: You're right. I'm going to get rid of the offending party now.

Types....

Brattybitch4u has been blocked

I growl out my frustration and rub my temples. I'm too old for petty drama in a non-relationship relationship. It's been eight months on both sites, yet I've had my fair share of headaches on Sweetsugar. I wasted so much on Theresa, obviously a disobedient super brat. I wanted to take care of her, but I also wanted her to make me feel good emotionally and seem interested in me and not just for my money. But she was one of many failed connections as a sugar daddy.

My inbox was full of messages after adding a few more recent pictures and a bit more to my bio, adding my emphasis on wanting a girl with a brain and not just a body.

Of course, no one reads the bio, they only go by what I look like. Nobody was building a solid foundation for anything. That's what went wrong with Tiffany, Brittany, Jem, Sierra, and Dominique.

I found out that Tiffany was married with three kids, not estranged, or divorced either. In fact, her husband came in while we were on one of our explicit video chats. He threatened to kill me if I ever contacted his wife again before the line was disconnected. Her profile also disappeared soon after.

My search on Brittany led me to find out she had four sugar daddies, including me. She wasn't the least bit remorseful when I confronted her, and she said I was easily replaceable.

Jem just didn't keep the conversation going; she was sweet and could even be a decent sub with some work, I wasn't able to dedicate that type of time. Dominique's background showed she had a warrant out for a hit and run from two years ago. I tipped off the cops on her whereabouts.

And then there was Sierra. She crossed the line when she did a federal background check on me. The agency gets notifications when our aliases are run through any database. She had her friend in the FBI run the check but couldn't find anything.

That's because Colin Wentworth doesn't exist. There's a reason why I introduce them to Colin instead of Daniel. They both want a genuine connection, but Colin is like the bodyguard of the heart, Daniel's been locked up so long he's vulnerable to get hurt so Colin sniffs them out. And so far, he hasn't found someone worthy enough to allow Daniel to come forward.

What did it matter that she ran a background check? I knew she wouldn't get so much as a blip from it. This was not going anywhere, and I knew it, I was going through the motions. I didn't feel a need to know her and that was critical.

She put the nail in the coffin when she tried to reverse search my pics. My agency had the technology to block and erase all that info. When all her efforts were exhausted, she tried to get me on a video call. After the Tiffany incident, I limited video chats to only those who had potential.

Sierrasloane: I want to see you.

Killerinstinct69: We're not there yet.

Sierrasloane: Fine! Then I'll find someone who doesn't keep secrets from me.

Killerinstinct69: So be it.

Sierrasloane: You probably have a small dick anyway.

You can no longer receive messages from this user

No skin off my back. I delete the conversation and move on.

After so many failures, I started to think, was this for me? Maybe an assassin is supposed to be a lone wolf.

After hanging out with Vincent and having a set of twins end up in my bed, I made up my mind to quit the site. I didn't care if Vincent found out. After kicking them out, I opened my laptop and logged in.

I had a few girls add me to their likes on Naughtyfet, I would have to see what kind of interests they have, especially the submissive interest.

After that, I humored myself by going through the Sweetsugar notifications one last time before I deleted my profile. Then I saw someone liked my page and left me a message:

Kittenwantstoplay: Hi.

One word, but that one word sparked my interest for some reason. She wasn't trying too hard or anything of that nature. She just said hello.

Before replying, I click her icon for her profile and come face to face with a stunning beauty with golden tone skin and brunette wavy hair. She had some pics with straight hair or braided away from her face but mostly that beach waves look. She had flawless skin and a smile full of curiosity. A smile that would make your day that much brighter. I assumed her profile picture to be a high school graduation photo with her adorned in academic ropes indicating she was an honor student.

I wonder if she was valedictorian or salutatorian, not many others around her had ropes or cords on their deep burgundy gowns.

If she hadn't messaged me, I would have gladly quit this site ten minutes ago, but there was something about this girl. I scan her profile stats; it looks like she's just over the legal threshold. I usually went for older, like being able to buy your own drink, legal, but I replied:

Killerinstinct69: Hi, you are stunning. Were you an honor graduate?

I failed to realize the green dot until I saw those three gray dots indicating she was typing.

Kittenwantstoplay: Thank you and sharp eye! I was class salutatorian, the winner beat me by one point, she had a 4.3 GPA, and I had 4.2. Suck up, ha, kidding.

Oh my god, she was practically a genius. What was this angel doing on a site like this? There had to be more.

Killerinstinct69: Congratulations, well deserved.

Kittenwantstoplay: Thank you. So, how has your day been or your night?

She seems nervous but it was nice to be asked about me.

Killerinstinct69: It was good, had to work earlier, but glad to be relaxing now. Found a nice scotch to indulge in.

Kittenwantstoplay: Scotch burns something awful!

Looks like she's been indulging in things she shouldn't be.

Killerinstinct69: Why are you drinking scotch, young lady?

I saw those dots cycle a bit longer than before.

Kittenwantstoplay: I tried some at a party. So, I read your bio, and I see you want meaningful conversation, but what else?

I see she's trying to steer the conversation elsewhere and I find it funny. I decided to humor her since she said she read my bio. She's already light years ahead of the other girls I've dealt with.

Killerinstinct69: That's the bulk of it. I've been on the site for a while and all the girls are the same: empty, boring, and begging for money. I get the site's premise, but I also want a connection more than monetary or physical. The money can come later, but only if I find you intellectually stimulating.

Kittenwantstoplay: Makes sense. Hopefully, you find me stimulating. ;)

I imagine her voice dropped a few octaves to sound breathy and needy. Hell yes, she stimulated me! Almost too much as I look down.

Killerinstinct69: Absolutely, kitten. Tell me about yourself.

Kittenwantstoplay: Well, I'm 18, graduated high school from Greenview in the Miami suburbs. About to attend the University of Miami in the fall. Major currently unknown.

Killerinstinct69: With those aspirations and your beauty, you could get any man you wanted.

Kittenwantstoplay: Aww thanks, but I need more than the typical guy/girl relationship. I thrive when I'm being cared for and for most guys that's more than they can handle. Me as a normal functioning college student is a mask to who I really want to be,

which I'm still figuring out. I have some curiosities I'm looking into...

Interesting. I'd like to know exactly what type of attention she needs and if I could provide that.

I might have died and gone to heaven. Everything about this girl intrigues me. I want to help; I don't want to see her struggle or have to turn to some other man. I can feel Daniel perked up at our interest in this girl. Her vibe is a breath of fresh air.

Kittenwantstoplay: So, tell me about you! This goes both ways.

Killerinstinct69: Well, I just turned 41. I travel quite a bit for my job in umm...sales. I have a best friend who made me join this site to "loosen up," and it's been a nightmare until this moment.

Kittenwantstoplay: I'll assume that's due to me so, thanks for the compliment.

Killerinstinct69: You're welcome.

My phone buzzed annoyingly with my next assignment interrupting this perfect conversation. Looks like one of our most wanted, the self-proclaimed "Prince of the Boston Street Kings" and some other crime families were in Boston for a scheduled secret meeting.

Killerinstinct69: I hate to cut this short, duty calls. I have to catch a flight ASAP.

Kittenwantstoplay: Ok, well, nice to virtually meet you and safe travels.

Killerinstinct69: Nice to meet you, too...uhh, I didn't get your name, beautiful?

Kittenwantstoplay: Everyone calls me Emmy.

Killerinstinct69: I'm... Colin. Sweet dreams, Emmy.

I catch myself smiling as I log off.

She is memorable, I am sure she will be in my dreams and fantasies in the near future until we can chat again. But now I need to focus on Bobby Vianetti, the *clown* prince of the Street Kings. He was a pompous, arrogant, territory-hungry son of a bitch. Everyone knew he was heir to the throne after his father, Carlos.

When you live in the light of your indiscretions and have a target on your back every day this wasn't one of those 'look forward to retirement' gigs, their role was even more dangerous than my job. But Bobby was cocky, he deemed himself untouchable, but I was coming to show how easy it was to get rid of the trash.

Ember (Emmy)

"Emmy! Are you group dating with us tonight?"

No, Kayla, because I don't have any prospects. I'm a bitter, lonely woman at the moment.

I roll my eyes then fix my face. "Not tonight, doll face." I hear her open my door over the soothing music in my headphones and plop down on my bed. I push one side off my ear.

"What's wrong?" I could hear the concern in her voice; she's like the group mom.

"Nothing's wrong; I'm taking some time to spend alone. Go out and have fun for me, okay?"

She huffs, "Fine, but we will talk about this tomorrow."

Of course, we will, mom.

"Yeah, yeah...tell the guys I said hello and maybe I'll join next time."

"The day you have a steady boyfriend again or even a potential one, I'll shave my head."

Rude.

I shake my head as she exits my room. She's right; I don't keep interested long. I crave more. Yes, I am on a sugar baby site, only because my roommates hassled me until I created a profile in front of them. Then they harassed me until I saved a few potentials and then again until they saw me go out a few times. They are openly on the site because the men help pay the house bills, sometimes they sleep with them, and sometimes they don't. For example, Carla & Millicent are in platonic-only relationships with much older men who only want to show them off around town. They pay for their time. Sex is not on the table, and they are free to get that elsewhere.

For me, I wanted a connection that wasn't connected to money. I needed someone who wanted to care for me and look out for me. After a long day of studying at the library or researching in the archives, I want to come home, have him undress me, and use his strong hands to wash me and massage the stress away. I read something that said I had submissive qualities and that I needed a dominant to provide that feeling of being taken care of.

Well, I'll tell you right now, they are not on Sweetsugar. The last few guys were the pick of the litter.

There was Kent, the spoiled rich man-child. At the age of 37, all he talked about were his stocks and exotic trips around the world, although he never offered to take me. He was so into his own stories he couldn't see the sheer boredom on my face. I found myself openly rolling my eyes, but he loved to hear himself talk. I have a sneaking suspicion it was his parents' money he was flaunting.

After that disaster, I tried to stay off the site, but they insisted, and I met Dorian... the secret convict. I only found out about that when Carla ran across his latest arrest in the local jail log.

I wondered where he disappeared to.
Prison...it was prison.

Dembe, was into some weird shit. Everyone is entitled to their curiosities, but this was way beyond my comfort zone.

And then there was Brad; he was the icing on the cake when he told me that he owned me. That I should be available to him at all times. Whenever he wanted for whatever he wanted.

And don't get me wrong, I show as much attention as given, but he made me sound like a readily available piece of ass and nothing more. He made me feel cheap and he once told me I was too old to be on this site. I was 20 at the time and so from then on, I've just lied to seem younger. I hate that I let the insecurities of a 45-year-old man get to me.

But for men, 18 is the prime number right when we finally cross the legal threshold. It's when men think we're the most nubile, our breasts firm and perky, our asses high and full and our pussies are tight as a vice grip. They think they even have a shot at claiming the illustrious V card.

Well, minus my V card, I still have all that at 21 and beyond. I hate judgmental chauvinistic men and I was planning on leaving the site until I saw a profile I hadn't seen before. He popped up under the 'people you may like' section.

He was handsome, very handsome. He had a jawline sculpted by Michelangelo himself. His wavy hair swept back, and he was sporting a goatee and some stubble. It was a side profile somebody took of him mid-sip of his drink, but even from that, I could see he radiated a sexiness that intrigued me. I opened his profile and started reading, his looks were already there, but I needed to see if we clicked on a mental level.

I see he's in his 40's, around the same age as Brad, but not a deal-breaker, as long as he thinks differently. He didn't list a location and kept his search to the entire country; he must have money or is an avid traveler. According to his interests, he is very adamant about intellectual conversation. I'm glad to see he knows what he wants. I can imagine the airheads he's encountered.

He has 567 people following him and has over 2k likes; ooh, I see he's got a couple of stalkers who liked and commented under all his pictures. Whoever this brattybitch is, she's possessive. Let's see if he's messing with her.

If he is hers, she will answer for him very possessively and quickly. The girls here can be cut-throat, especially the self-labeled brats.

Well, I'll say hi, no underlying message, just to feel him out.

I send it and look for a movie on Netflix to watch while my roommates have a date night. I change into my PJ shorts and top before I hear a ping from my computer. I lay down to read his message and smile; he thinks I'm pretty. He must have clicked on my profile picture because he asked about my graduation cords, which is interesting.

Our conversation is light and casual. He emphasized his need for a stimulating discussion, so I decided to tease and ask him if I stimulated him. He said I did and called me kitten.

When he calls me kitten, I have flashbacks to the last two times I tried to experiment with my daddy kink. I've been burned twice, and I don't have the energy but when he says it, I feel butterflies.

Then, because I am enjoying myself, he has to go abruptly, and I am saddened.

It's been one conversation, Ember, sheesh.

But why do I sort of miss him already?

Colin

Tonight's kill is a two-for-one special. The bounty was $500,000 for one or $750,000 if I eliminated them both. I planned for a double kill shot with a single bullet; it's like the assassin version of the hat trick. The venue was a dining hall at a top-tier elite country club. The hall had floor-to-ceiling glass windows looking out onto the lush green and forest, but it also made it easier to find the perfect angle to set up, the darkness of night shielding me.

After 11 pm, they had conducted most of the meeting business. I scribbled down a few notes for the agency to update the profiles of the other crime families, the business they may be conducting, and new faces we may not be aware have joined the syndicate.

Now they were smoking cigars and drinking 25-year-old scotch and bourbon. I know my labels.

I located my two targets. Bobby laughed and had some ditzy girl in his lap, Carlos was next to him in the hot seat. It looked like he was giving some sort of speech to their guests. I had strict orders to take out Bobby and his dad, but it was a gold mine of the criminal elite. Someone could easily drop the national crime rate by eliminating this entire room, but that wasn't my assignment.

I switched up the twins for an SVD Dragunov semi-automatic. I used the scope's night vision to scan the perimeter for any outside security or bodyguards to take out, but I saw none; they must all be stationed inside.

Bobby's father raised his glass and turned towards his son, a smile on his face like a proud papa. He waved his hand while talking and Bobby rudely pushed the blonde over to the other seat and stood up, buttoning his coat before he shuffled over to his dad. The blonde doesn't look too pleased, but she didn't know that gesture saved her life.

I line up the shot, dead center of his dad's heart, until...Bobby hugs and claps his dad's back and they relish in their father/son moment.

I took that touching moment to send a bullet through the glass. It ripped through Bobby's back and into his dad's heart, they both jerked violently before they dropped. The blonde couldn't even scream, but once she saw she was covered in their blood splatter, she let out an ear-piercing shriek.

Everyone scrambled for cover as security burst through, but it was too late. I was already packed up by the time they started looking out the windows for the assailant... all the while thoughts of Emmy swirled in my head. She was something different, something special.

With two crime leaders executed and my assignment done, I complete my post-kill ritual.

I burn everything in the hotel's furnace and take a long shower before I use the hotel robe to cover up, no need for clothes. I close my eyes and dream of her.

It had been three weeks since I virtually met Emmy and every chance I've gotten to sit down I would check to see if she was online. Most of the time she was home, or she was getting back from the library. She was the sexiest bookworm I've ever seen. I had made the decision to bring up being exclusive. Daniel perked up when I thought about it. We haven't thought about that in a very long time.

I logged on and saw I had several notifications from that notyourdaddy19 girl and she also sent me a wink. If we become exclusive, I'll have to block her, right now she's harmless.

I got a text that there may be a job in Vermont, so I packed my bags, laid out my non-suit travel clothes, and waited for my flight info. Meanwhile, I get a ping.

Kittenwantstoplay: Hi.

Killerinstinct69: Hi, pussycat. What are you up to?

Kittenwantstoplay: The same boring thing, coming back from the library. You probably think I'm a big nerd.

Killerinstinct69: I do but it's the sexiest thing about you. Say, I wanted to ask you a question. We've been casually talking, and I want to know if you feel comfortable exploring your daddy kink with me. I'd love for you to be my princess.

Kittenwantstoplay: Really?!

Killerinstinct69: Absolutely and maybe eventually we'll look into other things we might

want to try out. Now I'm curious, where do you live? You don't have to give me an exact location.

Kittenwantstoplay: I live in Pompano Beach, north of Miami. I remember your profile doesn't have a location. I guess that means you're not in the same place for a long time? :(

I hate these conversations because they could go two ways: they are instantly turned off or pretend to be okay with it but then use it as a point to argue. So, I always answer carefully.

Killerinstinct69: I go where my assignments are and because they come at any time, it doesn't make sense to put down roots yet. I've been doing this for quite some time, and it works for me.

I brace for it, to be friend-zoned or dumped altogether. Daniel is nervous but Colin knows better and readies his cold response.

Kittenwantstoplay: Well, that makes sense. Why waste money when you can save what you make and stay in a hotel. Shame, it takes the curiosity out of seeing how your man lives, though. I wonder what your place would look like, like how would you style it?

Isn't she adorable?

Killerinstinct69: Well, you can see my hotel room if you want to… as far as style, probably something chic and simple I suppose. So, can I see and hear my princess in real-time, or is it too soon? Your call.

The conversation dots cycle for a moment.

Kittenwantstoplay: Wait just a moment…

I can't believe I asked to see her already, I didn't even hesitate. I check myself to make sure I look decent. Maybe I should wear a shirt since I am just in my robe.
Decisions, decisions…

Emmy

He wants to see me! I look down at my ice cream cone pajamas and suddenly I feel like I'm 12. I need something sexier but also look like I'm not trying. So, I slip on a mustard yellow gown and matching robe, simple yet cute. I check my hair and smile before replying that I was turning my camera on.

When I clicked his video chat request, I was met with the most gorgeous panty-dropping smile. He is way more handsome than his profile picture. I would do anything for him to run his hand down my spine. I gave him a nervous smile while looking, his gaze was so intense I had to look away.

What is this?! I'm usually more confident! His aura is so strong through the screen. It screams out dominant and I love the bluntness of very dominant men, it brings out my natural submissiveness.

I attempt to focus, noticing he's in a robe and I think it's just a robe. It gives me a peek at his chest. Heaven help me...

"Hello, little one."

My entire body temperature shot up 20 degrees. His voice reverberated down between my legs and I had to clench to stop the pulsing. Certain pet names make me feel so special, so protected. That was one of them.

"Hi, Colin."

My mind flashed to spanking her ass red for calling me by my name. We're in a learning phase so I let it slide this time.

"Ah ah ahhh, that's not what you call me. I guess we'll need more practice now, won't we?"

I whimper, holding my head down, "Yes, daddy, I'm sorry."

"Hey, look at me. You have nothing to be sorry for; this just happened. We're both learning from each other, feeling each other out, okay? Now let me see that beautiful face."

I perked right up and felt my cheeks flush. His eyes looked at me with such adoration.

"So, is my little one ready for college?"

I felt my lip quiver as I quickly tried to answer without hesitation. It felt like an interrogation. "Umm, yeah. I, uh, I'm excited and nervous. I heard it's a lot different from high school, but I have my girlfriends."

It was a little white lie. I know that it's frowned upon, and I could get punished for lying. I'm not 18 nor a freshman, but I still wasn't sure if he thought like Brad; like I was already past my prime for a site like this, I couldn't take more verbal abuse, so I'll play the role and deal with the consequences later.

"Don't worry. You'll fit right in."

I heard what he said, but I had this nagging question repeating over and over in my head.

"Daddy, have...have you been a daddy before?" It was a sensible question especially if we transition into the more traditional DDlg style, including the establishment of his rules. But I couldn't help wondering if I was his one and only princess.

"No, you would be my first, for that and probably anything else you want to try. I'll do some research on this fetish site I've been referring back to. You should look; they have a lot of information for beginners. It's called Naughtyfet. Have you had a daddy before?"

I should have seen that coming. I hate that he can't be my first. He probably wouldn't get such a shell of my former self.

"Yes, two of them and they were bad daddies. That's why I haven't explored it with anyone else." I didn't want to go into detail, and he sensed it.

"It's okay. I will try my best to keep you happy. I'm in no rush, this doesn't have to be about sex if you don't want it to be. I can be content with a platonic relationship; there will never be any pressure to go further. You're safe with me."

You're safe with me.

He doesn't know how much that means to me. I just want to feel appreciated and cared for. The fact that he brought up being my daddy was shocking, I was going to feel him out, but it feels right.

"Emmy? Hey, you zoned out over there, are you okay?"

"Hmm? Oh yeah, sorry I got lost in thought."

He licked his lips and flashed his smile.

"Give me your number."

"Ok, do I get yours, too?"

"When I call you, you'll have it, but my number changes quite a bit. You'll have to answer any number you don't recognize because it might be me."

What kind of sales is he in?! I mean this IS Miami. He really sounds like...

"Are you a drug dealer?!"

44

Shit! What a great start, Emmy!

I didn't mean to yell; I slapped my hands over my mouth. He raised his brow, but said nothing, it was like he was feeling me out or letting me suffer for my little outburst. If it were either of my other Daddies, that would have been an automatic punishment. I brace for him to raise his voice, but he chuckles, breaking the awkwardness.

"No, I don't deal drugs. There's a reason I can't disclose a lot of detail, but I assure you it isn't drugs."

He sounded so sincere. If it wasn't dangerous or life-threatening, I guess it was okay. I gave him my number, but he didn't program it into his phone. He taps his temple and says he remembers and doesn't need to because he won't be using that phone after tonight and he'll call me from the new one when he's settled. He's so old school with a phone call when a text is so much faster.

But the whole phone situation is weird, right? I don't say anything, but I do interrupt our conversation by yawning suddenly. I've been studying too late and too hard.

"Oh, looks like it's time for my tired little kitten to go to bed."

"But I want to stay on longer. Please?" Another yawn, solidifying his stance. "Don't talk back, what I say goes, that'll be the first established rule. I only want what's best for your well-being. Besides, you need your beauty sleep. I promise we'll talk again. Sweet dreams, my beautiful girl."

I concede when he calls me his. I'm so exhausted, but I give him a small smile. "Sweet dreams, my handsome daddy."

Colin

Nine months have passed since we became exclusive.

Emmy and I talk when I'm not on assignment, reading up on my targets, and when she's not in class.

We've been sending each other articles about the dom/sub lifestyle. She says she really likes Naughtyfet and all the forums, she is immersed in the submissive forum and the playpen of pets. Apparently, she likes pet play as well. She says she prefers Naughtyfet to Sweetsugar. We only use it for the hands-free video chat option.

It's hard to keep up with this Colin charade, but I have to, for her safety. I need to find a way to make her understand why I introduced her to Colin instead of Daniel. Why I constantly lie, keep secrets from her, and basically catfish her by presenting Colin as my true self. If Daniel were personified, he'd be shaking his head in disappointment and to be honest, I feel like I am letting him and her down.

Emmy and I have leveled up to sexual play over video chat and to say she is amazing is a serious understatement.

I've done some research on the basics, including what my rules might be, submissive posture and positions, and applicable punishments. It's hard trying to explore while entirely online, but she has made an effort to please me in every way.

I still reminisce about the last session; it did not start well. I missed a video chat with her but not on purpose.

It was after one of my assignments, I was going to trash the previous burner, so I quickly texted her from the new one.

Me: New phone, kitten. Twenty minutes.

E: Okay.

I thought that gave me enough time to shower, change, then go down and find the incinerator to torch the evidence. But I had to wait for the elevator, which was slow, and I was on the 10th floor. Then I had to take the stairs down from the first floor. So, by the time I returned, I had missed her calling me because it had passed the 20-minute mark. She left a crying emoji in our chat.

My little pussycat, so needy. I love her eagerness to be in my presence, to be so happy to see me on the screen.

I call back and I am met with a not-so-happy face. I think she's pouting. I better douse the flames.

"Princess, I was wrapping up some important details. I wasn't ignoring you."

"Hmph!" She looks away, sticking her nose in the air.

Well, I guess she wants me to bring out my dominant side.

"I guess someone wants to be a bad girl. You want to be punished for ignoring daddy? Maybe I should make you watch me jerk off while you're not allowed to touch yourself, look away, or log off. Is that what you want?" I lean forward resting my arms on my legs, staying quiet so she knew that I was serious.

She turns back around, her eyes as big as saucers. I'm slightly distracted as her breasts sway from the sudden movement. I can't wait to feel those against me, I can't wait to feel her against me period. Then she brings me out my thoughts when she gasps.

"No, I'm sorry! Can we play, please?"

I sigh as I lean to the side, contemplating and I could see she was waiting anxiously for an answer. She plays on my weakness and my need by biting her lip.

"I suppose. First, how was your night?" She had gone out with her roommates to some club downtown, you know, typical young adult behavior. I'm way past that stage.

She stretches and huffs, "Well, the club was packed and smelled like cigarettes, I'm glad I was able to wash it out of my hair. Then, I got hit on by six guys and groped by one while I was dancing, and he was behind me…"

I zone out knowing some stranger touched what's mine and I'm not happy to hear it. I don't feel right punishing her with my indiscretions. So, some guy touched her? She was here with me now. I tune back in, "thankfully you buzzed me. I took that time to take an uber home, shower, and put this on for you…I hope you like it." She purrs sending chills that made me even harder.

Her view gets a bit wobbly as she sets up her camera and steps back. Her dangerous curves are accentuated by royal blue lace, her breasts overflowing the delicate fabric caressing her beautifully toned skin. She perched on her bed, her hands clasped together in front of her, making her arms squeeze her chest further together.

She's going to be the death of me, but what a way to go, I tell you!

A low growl slips my lips as I skim over her entire body; she knows what she does to me. She slides against her silk sheets until she's laying on her side, facing me. Her bed hair makes her look even sexier.

"I want to see it. Show me what I do to you when I wear pretty things like this for you, daddy. Just for you."

"Are you asking or are you telling me?" I raise my brow causing her to whimper and lower her head.

While she wasn't looking, I was able to slip off my shirt, trying to give her a dose of her own medicine and it worked when she looked up finally and I saw her squeezing her thighs to dull the throbbing between her legs.

She remains still on her bed, silently begging me to tell her what I want her to do.

We have experimented with several role-playing options, but honestly, being herself works for me. I play whatever she wants me to because I enjoy seeing her happy. She doesn't even have to say what her intentions are; her body language says it all. And I can read her like a book.

"Daddy dom wants to see his kitten all dressed up. Two minutes...go."

She turns to dig in her nightstand, her ass on full display, the lace hugging the ampleness. I fantasize listening to her moan in desperation for me when I place a good lick on it.

She sets her solid black kitten ears on her head and her fingerless fuzzy gloves that look like paws. She looks at me to confirm the final piece of her costume. "No tail this time, looking at you right now and I'm ready to explode." She's still a novice at the tail plug and I can tell it causes her a bit of discomfort. She says it takes repetition and she really wants to go all-in when it comes to embodying her inner kitten.

She bends down, resting her head on her hands with her ass in the air. Feeling the almost unbearable throbbing, I rip my sweats down, exposing the red tip to the chilly air, making it more sensitive. I lick my hand and wrap it around my hard, thick cock. Our eyes connect as soon as I start to move up and down. She licks her lips hungrily, shifting to lie on her back as she takes the phone and gives me an aerial view. One hand holding the phone, the other grazing her collarbone with the tips of her fingers.

I continue to stroke myself while watching her lust over me. "Purr for me, I want to hear my irresistible sex kitten."

Her purrs send chills down my spine, it's primal, animalistic, and it turns me on so much more. Then she teases further by pulling the top of her bodysuit down, wrapping her arms under her breasts, and squeezing.

I watch her slip her hand between her legs. "Can I?" She whispers softly and I know she's soaking wet for me. "Go ahead." I say firmly and watch her intently.

"Daddy..." It slips from in between her breathy moans; she's desperate, desperate to feel the knot unravel and to send herself into climactic bliss.

I imagine I can taste her on my fingers, I need her confirmation. "Show me how wet you are, then taste yourself." She smirks when she holds up her two fingers.

She was absolutely soaked.

Then she licks them, "Mmm, I wish you could taste me." I stroke harder as the tingles from my balls shoot up my spine as I groan. "Pussy cat...what are you doing to me? I'm so fucking close. I want to cum with you screaming my name."

Her fingers slide in and out with her thumb dialing up her orgasm on her clit. Her breasts sway back and forth, her back arches as I simultaneously feel that sign, the sign of an explosive climax. I squeeze my balls to pause the sensation shooting through them, prolonging my pleasure.

She watches me like a horny teenager watching their first porno. Then she shuddered before looking away, her eyes shut.

"That's it, imagine me in between your legs, licking, caressing, and teasing your aching pussy. Just before you reach climax, I slam into you. Oh, you're squeezing me so good, baby. So fucking tight, I can feel you pulsing all over me...are you going to cum for daddy?"

She's so wrapped up in the pleasure she doesn't answer me. I drop my voice, lower and deeper. "Answer me, kitten. I shouldn't have to ask you twice." I slow my strokes because as much as I would like to orgasm together, I enjoy watching her fall apart.

"Ye-ye-yessss! I... I need it. Say it, say it to make me cum."

I have no idea why it triggers her so hard, but it does. I suppose it's her overactive imagination in play since we have yet to physically meet. So, I oblige. "Use me, kitten, and ride me until your legs shake, your pussy aches, and you cum all over daddy." And that's all it took for her body to give in.

"Yes...oh god yes, mffmgh!" I resumed stroking and watching her aftershocks. Knowing I had caused her immeasurable pleasure sent me over the edge as I came. Her eyes pooled in lust as she licked her lips, amazed at all that I gave.

"Oh…." I exhale hard; I was spent.

She is now the main reason I stay in the gym; this was exclusively online yet, I'm exhausted. To be fair though, I did have a flight and an assignment this morning. But most credit goes to her; she keeps me young and virile.

But enough reminiscing...

I shake my head, trying to get back into the present and my assignment, but I know the moment I'm free and in Miami, I'll have her climbing the walls, crying out my name. My dominance is eager. She already sounds so needy and wanting when she screams my name, but I needed to focus on the current portfolio in front of me and not my memories.

"Open your dossier. This is Marco Giovanni Banetti, one of the Società Segreta of the Sacra Corona Unita."

"In English, Socrates." After a cross-country flight, it's too late to try and decipher Italian.

"He's one of, if not the prince of the fourth mafia. They only class them; they do not identify who heads the table. Only a select few hold the title of Società Segreta, which is identified as their top tier."

"Why is he on our radar?"

"Banetti's been leading the way in arms, drug, and human trafficking, money laundering, extortion, and political corruption in this state. Rumor has it he's responsible for the Missouri run-off election and subsequent double recount. Intelligence reports believe that Banetti is eyeing the Presidential election, greasing palms to continue his operations without having to worry about American law enforcement at any level. He's responsible for that horrific factory fire four months ago that killed 120 women and 47 children because of the illegally locked doors? All were trafficking victims from who knows where. They're still trying to identify victims by DNA analysis and match them against the missing database to contact their families. It could take another year."

"How much time to complete the mission?"

"In 24 hours, better within 12. Intel suggests he may be returning to Italy and reverse trafficking women for his slimy associates over there. Forced weddings and much worse, especially because he's known to drug them."

I had heard enough. "Done."

"You're the best of our best, Zeus. Make an example of him. You have permission."

In our expertise, there are two types of assignments: the quick and quiet ones and the ones that make even the most veteran of reporters cringe when reading the details.

I'm given the latter and I was going to enjoy making an example of him.

Every assassin chooses a signature weapon to mark their kills. For me, it's the twins. For Hermes, he prefers to make his statement loudly with a double barrel sawed-off shotgun. Ares' precision is with a crossbow, you'd think that would be an archaic weapon, but he can hit his target between the eyes from 200 feet away. I think he was born with one in his hand; his accuracy is unmatched.

Poseidon chose hand-to-hand combat mastering kukri blades with his signature red and gold tsukaito handles; he usually ended up bathed in his enemy's blood.

And finally, Athena with a pair of chrome Canik TP9SF Elite handguns and a backup butterfly knife passed on to her by her father, a legendary enforcer. She considers it her lucky charm.

Together, we receive assignments, execute them, get paid, and wait for the next job. We usually don't commingle unless we have a group assignment or are called somewhere for a meeting of sorts. And even then, we listen or respond to a voice, not a person. It works for me; I don't need to see who I work for as long as you pay me.

Back to Banetti, tonight he decided to visit a local super-exclusive strip joint alone in the Yellow Brick district, which consisted of a lot of factories turned into businesses. It was becoming increasingly popular with the city's crime families. They could conduct meetings or relax in these establishments that held secret rooms and password-protected areas.

I received the 24-hour password to get in and the code for the back rooms where he'd most likely be.

Decked out in my classic Emporio Armani black-on-black suit, I looked like I belonged there, waiting to conduct dark dealings with the scum of society.

I stroll in confidently, at the same time looking for where the back rooms would be. Set in the center of the venue was the main stage; two girls were dancing seductively together, grinding against each other, squeezing and caressing, riling up all the men who were mentally indulging their wildest threesome fantasies. They showed their appreciation by littering the stage in dollar bills and with a higher denomination offering, were rewarded with a quick feel of their ass or tits.

The other dancers were walking around giving lap dances to those eager to blow their paycheck to get rubbed against or even more to get special services in the champagne room.

I sat at the bar and observed the waitresses to see which one would reveal the way. Ten minutes later, a fiery redhead in a snakeskin vinyl miniskirt and nosebleed heels took a tray with a single scotch malt toward the stage but then made a quick left and disappeared.

Bingo.

As I stand up, pay, and tip the bartender for the shot of Johnny Walker Blue, she licks her crimson lips as her fingertips brush my hand, I wink to tease her. Definitely not my type but beautiful in her own way. I button my suit jacket and head toward the backroom. When I turn left, I'm in a short hallway and there's a security guy at the red-colored door. He looks like a moving brick wall, he's massive.

He stares down at me menacingly, "Password." He doesn't state it like a question but a command.

I clear my throat, hoping my voice doesn't crack like a prepubescent teen. I need to sound confident like I belong here. "Serendipity," I state.

He's stoic for a few painful seconds before he knocks on the door three times, and it is opened from the inside by a young lady sitting on a stool.

That throws a wrench in my plan, I didn't mind killing the bodyguard if I had to, but she looked to be Emmy's age. For a moment, I imagined it was her sitting on that chair. Tonight, I would have to use my backup plan, she's probably a student who needs to pay her way through college. I pass her and see several black doors with lights above them, red meant occupied and green was available.

I only saw one red light...Banetti had to be in there, but was he alone? Who's to say his minions weren't already there waiting on him. I wasn't sure, but anyone involved with him deserved to die anyway.

I selected the room after Banetti's, closest to the emergency exit, and saw the whole room was surrounded by two-way glass. It's a tactic for the owners to keep an eye on their investments. To them, the girls were fuckable property.

I'm alone in this cold, dingy room, there's a red velvet couch on one side and a stripper pole in the center of the room. I sit on the single folding chair in front of the pole. Then the door opens and a tall brunette walks in wearing silver glitter six-inch heels and not much else.

My kitten is not a brat, but she is territorial and would kill me if she knew I was here, work-related, or not. The girl starts her routine, swaying as she leaned against the pole. I immediately hold up five, hundred-dollar bills.

"Leave."

Her eyes shined at the money, but she also looked offended that I didn't want her to dance for me. She shrugged, took it, and slid it into her barely-there bikini top. "Whatever you say. If you want to jerk it alone, I'll leave you to it. Could have done that in the bathroom for free."

I internally laugh as I reach into my pocket for my glasses case. I slide them on and press the tiny button on the side that gives me the ability to see through the two-way glass.

I peer in to see Banetti getting a sloppy blow job from a curvy dancer and judging by the way he was slamming her down; he was just about done. She was fighting against his aggressive grip to breathe or get a break. He pulls her hair with a final grunt. Then he pushes her off him; she crumples to the ground as he throws money in her direction. She wipes him from her mouth and gathers the money.

"Get out! *Sporca puttana!*" (filthy whore) He spat at her and she looked enraged while gathering her discarded costume. "Fuck you, you filthy fucking pig!" She screamed back before slamming the door hard enough the walls shook, reflecting in the mirrored surface. He took that moment to light up a cigar to bask in emptying his balls for a fee.

Now was the time to strike. I set my watch for fifteen seconds as I punched a six-digit code on my phone. Then after the countdown ended, the electricity went out. Earlier, I placed a device on their breaker box that shuts off the power without any telltale signs.

I press the button on the side of my glasses again to add night vision. I see Banetti stand up and with no time to spare I aim and fire one eviscerator after another. The initial blasts through the glass into his kneecap and before he could react to the excruciating pain of the first, the second round splattered his skull and brains all over the room.

I knew someone had to have heard one if not both shots and the shattering of the massive glass wall, so I walked out cautiously.

I switched my clip to regular rounds, to wound not kill; as I heard security come through, I took them both down after the door shut behind them, further muffling the shots fired. Their bodies drop and the door girl screams, frozen in fear. I cover her mouth and inject her with a sedative. She'll wake up sore but won't remember much when the cops question her.

I slip out the back before anyone else comes, grab the blackout device, and jog back to my rental. I head back to my hotel to change, dispose of any evidence, and close the case. I feel the pulsing of my killers high and I'm ready to play.

At the stoplight before the hotel, I send a quick text:

M: Did you pay your bills, pussy cat?

E: Yes, daddy. I paid all my bills but...I don't have any leftover.

She was learning a valuable lesson in adulthood, learning to prioritize your bills and sometimes you don't have much left to cover the basics. I want to make sure she knows how important it is, of course, I could take care of them, but I want her to experience it. She screenshots all her receipts. I checked them as I was walking up to my room.

M: Good girl. I sent you a little reward for being so responsible.

I watch those three dots flash on my screen as I slide my keycard into the door until,

E: Thank you, but it's too much! I only wanted to buy a new bathing suit for you. It's a bright red, two-piece thong bikini I saw at this boutique.

That did it...I told her to log on so I can video chat and she answered on the first ring.

"Hi, daddy." There was so much sexual tension underlying the innocence in the tone of her voice.

"Hey. Why don't you use some of the extra money to get a new lingerie set for me, too? I can't wait to finally touch you."

"Me, too. I can't wait for you to make me all yours." She smirked mischievously.

I wanted that more than anything. I had two assignments in the past two weeks that landed me in Florida, but none close enough to visit, and I had another assignment that I had to take immediately after completing the first. Luck had not been on our side.

"I hope so, too."

Then I hear movement and see her girlfriends come into the background.

"Umm, thanks for knocking! Why are you guys in my room?" She sounds highly irritated as they come in unannounced; she angles the phone downward. That makes me wonder if they know about me. She angles it back up to look at me mouthing an 'I'm sorry.' Her brows are furrowed as she rolls her eyes. I see the girls walk back into her closet.

"When have we ever needed to really knock on your door before? It's time to have some sexy, night out on the town, fun! Us girls are going to Vellum. Get dressed; we leave at 10:30 pm. We're going to get dolled up so we can get dicked down! Personally, I'm looking for someone who can go all night, am I right?!"

They all whoop and holler, then I see a piece of shiny fabric tossed her way. I believe it's supposed to be a dress. She holds it up, it's way too short for my liking and she glances to see my disdain before quickly flinging it to the side. I can see the panic in her eyes when one of the girls stated their plans of going out to screw random guys and wanted her to tag along and join the festivities. Now, I'm really sure they don't know anything about me.

I didn't like what I heard at all. It was stirring up a part of me I keep hidden because it has no use when it's unleashed. That demon is jealousy.

"Guys, I'm not in the mood to go out. Miami nightlife is boring and all the guys our age are the same douchebags. I'm not looking to fuck some random guy."

They all stop moving. "Since when?! You've always been able to bag some poor victim if you want to. Face it; everyone wants to fuck you." Then they burst out laughing.

She lays the phone down, but I can still hear her shuffling and moving.

"That's enough! Get out!"

"Well, are you coming or not? You owe me for not going out last time."

I hear her sigh hard, "Yeah, fine."

I am not happy from what I heard, to know that sometimes she made a habit of randomly bedding guys in the not-too-distant past. She was way too young to have such a high body count, but jealousy created this random list of guys that was endless. I inhale and exhale deeply, trying not to let my demon show when she resumes our talk.

She's using you. She doesn't care; you heard her friends say everyone wants to fuck her. She probably fucks some random after getting off the phone with you. You'll never be anything more than her wallet.

My pessimism takes over all my thoughts and I try to keep from lashing out.

I look and her face says it all, mortification.

"Let me explain. It was a…"

I hold up my hand and she stops, whimpering at the abruptness. "You have somewhere to be. You should go get ready."

I lean back away from my computer screen putting cyber distance between us. I know I sound extremely cold, harsh, and emotionless, but I'm doing everything not to overreact. My demon had roared forward and the only way to stay in control was to end the call and take a step back.

"But it's not like that, I swear!"

Yeah, but was it before?

I sigh harshly and rub my eyes. "I'm exhausted. Go hang out with your friends. I'll talk to you later."

She flinched, unable to shield the pain on her face. She didn't even smile, she looked away, and that hurt before I ended the call.

Overly irritated, I switched back to a lethal assassin to take my frustration out on the heavy bag. I changed into my gym clothes and went downstairs.

I fabricated all these men in my mind. Those who had a chance to touch what was mine, caress what was mine, and watch her bounce up and down their lap as she cried out their name, not mine. Her beautiful, full lips sucking them off as they force her to deep throat every inch of them until they stand over her, shooting cum all over her as she sits submissively, smiling happily.

My jealousy demon was in control and out of control at the same time. I needed to isolate myself before I did something I would regret.

I am drenched in sweat when I return from a two-hour session. I shower then sit at my desk, contemplating breaking into the security system of that club she was going to. Was my kitten as innocent as she seems, or is it all an act?

Emmy

I was in no mood to go out before, but after the cold shoulder from Colin, I wasn't going to sit here and sulk. I try my best not to be a brat, but I was feeling so many different emotions I felt a need to act out. I need a distraction from his reaction.

Maybe this was my fault.

No, it was what Carla said about finding guys to fuck for the night and that everyone wanted to screw me, which isn't true! I probably sound like any other girl he met on that site. A money-hungry slut.

No! This is not my burden, it's his! I never once gave him the indication that I was that type of girl. He should trust and believe me. I'm his princess and I would never do anything to disappoint him.

I needed to take my mind off this. I was already mentally overloaded because I needed to create a study plan and break up the autonomy of the human body to make remembering easier. I was out of school but not yet in the program. There was so much pressure! It's all too much and now I had relationship problems and we didn't even have a solid talk about our status! Exclusive, yes, relationship, not sure.

Maybe dancing and drinking all night will take my mind from all this uncertainty.

How can he be so judgmental? I started to get angry, let's not forget he's withholding information from me!

How he never kept a phone or phone number, he wouldn't disclose where he was, and point-blank period, I didn't know what he did for a living! For all I know, he had a wife and three kids around here somewhere. Why should I trust what he says if he doesn't trust me?! If he wants to be disappointed in me, then so be it.

All my frustration came out as an ear-piercing scream into my pillow as Kayla came in and she paused when I pulled the pillow from my face.

"I was coming to see if you were ready or needed some help, but I feel like I walked into something serious. Want to talk about it?"

I needed to vent. I pat my bed and she sat gracefully in her little black dress. "There's something I've been keeping from you guys…" Just as I was about to come clean Carla, Millicent, and Tawny came strolling in looking hot and ready to paint the town, but their beautifully contoured faces fell once they saw my not-so-happy demeanor.

I gather my thoughts again. "What I was going to say was, I've been hiding a sort of relationship from you guys."

They all looked shocked, Millicent and Tawny sitting cross-legged on the floor and Carla on the corner of my bed behind Kayla.

"Why didn't you tell us? We would never judge you; obviously, we have no right to judge."

"I know it's just that, well, we were talking when you guys walked in earlier."

Carla gasped, "Oh my gosh! Did he hear us when I said we're going to find guys to fuck?"

I nod, "'Fraid so and the part about where everyone wants to fuck me. He shut down and was so cold before he ended the call. He's upset and probably thinks I'm some gold-digging whore and I..." I felt the tears start to build so I stopped.

Tawny shook her head. "Em, you are far from it! You are a certified genius, you graduated top of our class, and you're going to get into that umm...what kind of program is it again?"

"Kinesiology."

"Yeah, that. You have ambitions and goals! I am sure he needs to cool down, you know how fragile male egos are. Eventually, you can tell him that we were kidding."

Carla reaches over and takes my hand, "I'll even get on the call and tell him I didn't mean it! I don't want to ruin your relationship, Em."

"It's okay, Carla. I know you meant no harm. It's the way he shut down and put up the wall so fast; that's what hurt. It's almost like he personified his jealousy, that wasn't Colin. This is so stupid! We haven't talked about relationship status yet even after we started playing."

Millicent arched her brow, "Playing?"

Tawny nudges Milli's shoulder, giggling, "You know, like role play, age play, pet play. Honestly, I'd like a daddy myself, but all my potentials don't fit what I'm looking for, so I don't bring it up." She shrugs her shoulders and Milli "ahhs" in acknowledgment.

Tawny turns back to me, grinning like a Cheshire cat, "Now I'm curious as to what your play could be? What could our little Ember be into?" Tawny squealed and wiggled in excitement. I look around and they all seem to be interested. I was surprised at Tawny's little admission myself.

I felt the blush rise on my cheeks as I am about to admit. "I have a daddy kink and we do a bit of pet play. He has dominant tendencies, and he takes good care of me. I want to learn to be his submissive."

Tawny's eyes light up in excitement, "It sounds like he's the perfect person to explore it with. Let me take a wild guess. You give me… pussy cat vibes for pet play. Am I right?"

I purr proudly and she gives me a high five in victory.

"It's crazy, I've never felt comfortable trying pet play with anyone else but with him, it came as natural as breathing. I was reluctant to the daddy-dom play, too, with two failed attempts." Just thinking about both of them made me cringe.

"But there's still a lot of things I can't explain, like, I don't know what he does, and he is always traveling. I mean he can be in one place one day and the next across the country. It bothers me that he won't tell me, but he explains it's detrimental to his job. I don't even know what that means?! I like Colin so much but if he can't trust me with the basics, then why should I even bother?" I groan before burying my head in my hands.

Without warning, I clap my hands, surprising everyone. I stand up because if I didn't change the subject, it would turn into an all-night bitch fest, and we'd be eating ice cream and watching depressing rom coms. I didn't need additional shots to my heart.

"Okay, enough of the pity party, I can't do anything tonight and I want to dance my cares away. I will deal with Colin tomorrow, but tonight I want to have fun with my girls. Let me finish getting ready, okay? I can be done in 30."

Everyone agrees and dances eagerly out my door, but Kayla nods with a look I know too well. I know her, she's racking her brain to try to solve my problem. There wasn't an instant solution; I would have to let him come to me. I grab the little black dress thrown to me earlier, turn on my music, and prance into the bathroom. It was officially ladies' night! I ignore the wrench in my heart.

Colin

I'm trying to concentrate on my briefing, but I can't get these possessive, controlling thoughts out of my head. What is she doing to me? Colin wants to hack her security footage or her computer to see what she was doing. But Daniel feels guilty about how we reacted to what was probably innocent banter.

"Earth to Zeus!" I could hear Socrates' annoyance in the tone of his voice.

"Sorry, what were you saying?"

He sighs loudly, "Zeus, you've been taking direction from me for almost 20 years, we're like a team, and I'm your partner. In that time, I've learned a lot about you, and this is the first time you have been really distracted. Enough to interfere with your work."

In all that time, he's never said more than needed to know information before I made my kill. This was...odd.

"You're getting up in age, actually, I bet you didn't know but we're the same age. I bet you're contemplating what's next, I know I have. Most agents do, right before they notify us that they want to retire. This has been the longest you've been in a relationship and so things are probably getting serious. She's a classically pretty girl. You're going to need to stay fit for someone so young." He chuckles a bit.

What is going on?! How did this turn into relationship advice from my contact? Is this an episode of Dr. Phil? I ignored that last part, I didn't need to feed the beast.

"How do you know about her?"

That was a really stupid question.

"If we can crack international government multi-level cryptic servers, surely we can crack a website's pathetic firewall. We must keep an eye on all our agents, including their personal and social lives. We don't care what you do; we just make sure it doesn't interfere with your mission. And just so you know I do not go into your video chats. I'm sure you're not divulging secrets, so I let you have your alone time."

Well, that's good to know because it would be mortifying to know they watched us during one of our intimate sessions. I chuckle, "Must be weird to see I'm on these types of sites." I knew if they knew about Sweetsugar then they knew about Naughtyfet. He must think I'm a pervert.

"What makes you happy is none of my business unless it impedes your work or is illegal. I've seen some interesting things. If I could write a book. Anyway, Zeus, as you continue to contemplate what your life looks like on the other side of the fence, remember those who stuck by you through all the covert missions, late nights, phone calls, and hopping across the country."

Now I'm certain they've seen the text conversations between Emmy and me in the beginning and the ones we occasionally have when she's on her way to class or in the library. They see how different her chats were from the rest of the girls. I was more receptive to her; I didn't keep my answers short or clipped. No, I gave her all my time and attention when I could.

"Well...thank you for that; I think that's the first non-work conversation we've ever had. Okay, let's focus on my target... De something?"

"De Benzy, Mario. This is a different type of mission, still an execution, but he is a wanted international. His death will reach his home country and they'll be looking for retribution. The chances for retaliation could be high."

"Copy, Zeus out."

I scoff and shake my head to the very personal part of the conversation before I sit down and read my file.

Mario de Benzy, born in Spain and the equivalent of a socialite there but has a syndicate here to peddle his wares, including premium-grade ecstasy, heroin, and cocaine. He was another slimeball who used women and children for cooking, packaging, and distributing drugs around the Chicago tri-county area. He also ran most of the underground strip clubs, but there were rumors he was trafficking girls in and not legal-aged girls either. Rather teens that were taken from families of men who owed him any sort of debt.

Can you imagine the heartache of watching them take your child because you can't pay? Especially your innocent girl, so many frightening outcomes. He was a menace in his home country, and he was expanding over here.

Or so he thought.

Though I wanted to walk up and splatter his brains all over every surface, I would need a good amount of distance between us to avoid identification, so I perched on a nearby building, with my sniper rifle and jacketed hollow points waiting for him to exit his car. Everyone who emerges from his convoy would fall beside him. I would take out my frustration on them.

For a moment, I wonder what she is doing? Did she go out to the club and use her sexual prowess to get someone into her bed, or did she stay home waiting for me to break the silence? I could only speculate and that itself is dangerous.

Perched on top of an office building made of steel and glass, I angle my sight down to this mom-and-pop-style Italian restaurant that Mario is known to visit.

I picked this particular building as opposed to the others because they would be looking for the shooter in one of the windows before checking the roof; that's if I left anyone alive.

I wouldn't.

It's almost midnight, way too late for a normal operating restaurant which led me to believe that other dealings were happening in this innocent-looking establishment.

At 12:38 a.m., two heavily tinted black SUVs pull up and behind them, a white van. I see the driver of the van scan his surroundings before pulling his gun and going over to the other side to open the sliding door. His hand movements suggest he is yelling at someone, probably telling them to get out. While that is happening, the doors open on both SUVs and security jumps out, scanning the area, before coming around to the obstructed side to open the door.

It had to be de Benzy for such a thorough security sweep. I peered through my scope and aimed above the roof of the SUV. There was only a two-second window, maybe five, if he stopped for any reason. A distraction would seal his fate and I only had one chance. I slow my breathing and place my finger on the trigger waiting for my moment.

I heard a commotion from the van's direction but had to keep my focus on de Benzy. There was no movement for a moment, then a bodyguard went into the building. Probably to check it out before giving his boss the all-clear to enter. A few minutes later, the guy returns, stands a few steps from the SUV, and nods. Almost as quick as a flash, de Benzy steps out. Knowing what I know about crime families, most convoys were armored and adorned with bulletproof glass; it would be pointless to try and snipe him while he sat in the vehicle, my chance is when he steps out. He turns toward the van and flails his arms angrily, looking in its direction and that's my cue.

I don't hesitate to send three bullets that pierce his spine and skull. Before his security could soak in what happened, de Benzy staggers to the ground. I take each guard down with no more than two shots each. The 1st shot undoubtedly killed them. I was being thorough or venting my personal frustration.

I quickly looked over to see the van driver frantically trying to start the van to avoid the same fate. I took the chance and sent a round through the driver's side window, hitting him in the chest and causing him to slump over. The sound of the horn with the weight of his dead or soon-to-be-dead body echoed and bounced off the tall buildings.

Safe to say his car wasn't protected. Not surprised, they usually considered those who worked for them expendable and easily replaceable.

I scanned to see if I got everyone and am shocked to see five young girls in white sleep gowns, pressed against the restaurant wall, petrified by what they witnessed. I call the cops to the address and hopefully, they can get those girls back to their families. No doubt de Benzy was going to auction them off to the highest bidder.

We truly live in a sick twisted world.

I packed up and used the service entrance to make my way out of the building and to my car. My adrenaline was pumping, and I needed a sexual release badly. Then I remember and all those emotions basically kill my buzz. Jealousy was rearing its ugly head again. It was almost 1:30 in the morning here and she was an hour ahead. No doubt the main bar scene was closed, but what about the after-parties, or maybe they were soaking up their liquor with an early breakfast of carbs.

By the time I reached the hotel and did my routine, I looked to see no new messages from her, but she did upload several pictures from tonight.

Looks like they did go to Vellum, and she was in the VIP section. She wore that short, slutty dress given to her earlier. She had one picture by herself, hand on her hip blowing a kiss. It was flirty but it was innocent like the good girl I think she is. She wore sky-high heels that accentuated her amazing legs, legs I wish were wrapped around my head or at least propped open, teasing me with a front-row seat of her touching herself with my name spilling from her lips.

The following picture was a group photo. These must be her roommates I briefly saw earlier. They are all equally pretty, but she was the bright light, super sexy, and caring...

Now that I think about it, she was always asking how I was...

and how my day was going....

She made me laugh when I had a bad day and always told me how happy Daddy made her.

Goddamnit Colin!

I slam my hands down on the desk, making all the contents bounce and scatter all over and to the floor.

I pull at my hair, a coping mechanism for when I'm frustrated.

Daniel was frustrated at Colin. What was I thinking?!

She gave me everything I was asking for and never asked for more, never whined for more attention. She was content with what I gave her and I threw my emotional wall up and shut her off.

I pushed her away.

Maybe I wasn't emotionally mature to handle this. I needed to fix this but being apart meant I had to be creative. I found her address and sent four dozen roses, a bottle of champagne, and chocolate that would arrive tomorrow around six p.m. Romantic gestures Daniel would do to say he was sorry.

Emmy

I am never drinking again… I remember taking shot #6 and then we got a cab home, except for Tawny. She found a handsome brunette guy who asked her to dance and never let her go, that was a huge sign she was going home with him. I will get the juicy details later.

I look down and I'm still in my dress which is now more like a shirt. I groaned as I turned over to see it was noon and at the same time, my stomach made its intentions known that it needed food.

I slid off the bed to my feet to get into the shower. The warm water never felt so good; then, I shifted to cold to shock my body out of my hungover state. It opens your senses; I swear it works! Then, I slip on a deep V-neck silk maxi dress with floral detailing and head into the kitchen to have a late breakfast.

Later in the day, around 6 p.m., I was in the living room when the doorbell rang, and I heard Kayla say she'd get it. She must have ordered takeout again. I hope it's Thai.

"Oh my gosh!" She screeched and I immediately set my book down and shuffled to the front door. I was in total awe as three delivery men came in bearing the most beautiful roses. Two dozen were red, one was white, and another dozen in a beautiful lilac color. One of the men also had a gift bag in his hand.

"Oh Kayla, these are beautiful! Are these from that secret new guy you've been seeing?! He's winning points with me with a display like this!" All the other girls had gathered by the time they set down everything. The girls were also fawning over the display of affection.

"No, Emmy, these are for you. I just signed for it."

I felt like I was suddenly in a tunnel, her voice fading out. All I could hear was the thudding of my heart.

"For me? Wha...what?" She nodded and I could see the excitement on all their faces now as I walked towards the display. There was no card affixed to the flowers, but a card was in the bag that had champagne and chocolate.

Colin.

How did he even get my address? That little inquiry would have to wait.

I open the card:

Emmy, I shut down and made you feel unwanted and that's simply not true. Let me make it up to you tonight. Meet me on the site at 8 p.m. Bring the chocolate and champagne. I'm sorry, please forgive me. Colin.

They all squeal and swoon at the same time.

"Oh my gosh, that's so hopelessly romantic! Let's put the flowers in your room so he can see you got them. I'll go get the candles, too!"

"Tawny's right and you have less than two hours to get ready! Let's go. You got to get dolled up and sexy. What are you waiting for?! Go!"

I'm so overwhelmed it's as if I'm stuck in this moment. Whatever anger I was holding onto had faded and was replaced by the sweet smell of the roses. She was right; I needed to get ready.

Colin

I had showered and changed into my black silk pajama pants. The champagne was chilled by my bed. I set up the computer on my bed so I could sit against the headboard, giving her a full view of my chest and a bit lower to tease her. My hair was still damp, but that 'after shower' look was more irresistible than if I had walked through the door and taken off my shirt.

I was still a little early, so I went back to Naughtyfet and reviewed this article on 'Simple Rules to Establish in Your Dom/Sub Relationship'. Apparently, some doms are so strict they don't even allow their subs to speak freely. That's what works for them but personally, I don't want to hinder her from speaking her mind as long as it is respectfully. I will correct her if need be if she gets out of line.

The alarm on my watch goes off at 8 p.m. sharp. I log on and send her a video chat request and wait. I hope she has forgiven me or at least gives me a chance, but only time would tell.

As the seconds ticked by into minutes my demons were already whispering in my ear, darkening my mood, having me stew in my own tormented thoughts when she still hadn't logged on.

She's got her legs wrapped around some 25-year-old, muscle-bound blonde football player and he's devouring her pussy so good she forgot all about...

Ding

Her camera turns on and I see her bed with rose gold sheets covered in rose petals, one from each color I sent her, the box of chocolates was on the side, and a few lit candles around her bed, but she still wasn't in front of the camera.

"Emmy?"

I hear her sigh, "Since when do you call me that? You'd definitely punish me for calling you Colin, now, wouldn't you?" I couldn't see her, but I imagined her arms were crossed while she was awaiting my answer. Damn right I would, and I should punish her for being late and making me wait but then I remember why we were here in the first place.

"I was testing the waters. I couldn't punish you when I was the one who was wrong. I'm sorry for shutting down, kitten; it wasn't fair to you. Let's talk about it but not until you're in front of the camera."

She slides into view, lying on her side in a deep red silk slip that has a dangerously high split on one side, and both her legs are showing all the way up to her upper thigh. She looks mouth-watering. I instantly rub myself and sigh at the feeling of the cool silk against my warm, throbbing dick.

"Will you talk it out next time instead of shutting me out?"

"Yes, you got to understand this is the closest I've been to anyone in a long time." Or ever.

"I know..." She then lays on her back and I get a little side boob action before she brings her hands up to caress her curves, then runs her fingers through her loose waves. "Like what you see?"

"Yes, I do."

She's silent and she takes that moment to grab a piece of chocolate and bring it to her lips, kissing it playfully before biting sensually and moaning to the sweet confection melting in her mouth.

I feel my dominance emerging. He wants to play. I shift, sitting up a bit higher against the bed, my pajamas sliding lower just above my pubic bone. She licks her lips and flashes a side smile that sends him rushing forward.

"Strip. Now."

I saw her eyes widen and darken lustfully. She faces away, sitting up on her knees, crossing her arms in front of her as her hands grab the sides of the gown. I lean forward a bit more as the silky fabric skims over her soft curves, teasing me with her peep show. It revealed the roundness of her ass in matching burgundy lace boy shorts. I followed the garment up the curve of her back, revealing a small tattoo under the bottom of her matching bra. She pulls the fabric over her shoulders and head. She tossed it to the side and her hands were crisscrossed over her shoulders when she turned around, hiding her full, shapely breasts.

Someone's being a tease, but I am in control. I'm going to see if she's been reading the material I've been sending her and my suggestions.

"Modified position one, now."

Position one is on her knees, hands palm up on her thighs and her head down. Modified meant she could keep her head up. I wanted to incorporate it into our playtime to see if she was submissive.

Her eyes never left mine as she dropped her hands to her thighs, revealing a very sexy bandage corset bra. There were delicate straps of fabric crossing across her breasts like a cage.

Fuck, she looked irresistible! "My, my, my, what a delicious surprise for me. This one may be my favorite so far."

She didn't know how desperately I wanted to hear her call me Daniel as she came all over me.

I shook my head when I realized I was daydreaming, and she was waiting patiently. She didn't even interrupt me. She was a living fantasy right in front of my eyes.

"Sorry, pussy cat, I was thinking about what I would do when I finally got you in my arms. You may release from position one and get comfortable."

She blew two of the three candles out to create a soft mood lighting, very sensual as the remaining light outlined her body. Then she lay flat, angling her monitor down a bit.

"Ooh, tell me. If I was at your hotel door right now, what would you do?"

I stayed silent for a moment, building up the sexual tension, then I let out a low growl. "I'd grab you by the neck, pulling you in. Ripping your coat away, revealing to me the very sexy number you have on now. You gasp as I slam you against the nearest wall, then spin you around, pulling you against me. Kissing your shoulder, up to the nape of your neck, and then spinning you back around to kiss you intensely when I press you up against the window. You gasp as you react to the chill of the glass on your back, but it doesn't dull the inferno between your legs. I turn you once more and now you watch me peel everything off you from the window reflection as it pools to the floor. I take in your dangerous curves, your beautiful skin, and the way you eye me hungrily through the window. I'm going to let the world watch as I devour you..."

She bites her lip; I look over to see one hand caressing her breast and the other one mysteriously out of view.

What a naughty little pussy cat I have. I didn't tell her she could touch herself but it's so deliciously sexy I didn't want her to stop.

"More, daddy... tell me more." She begs me while squeezing her nipple and crying out. I couldn't take it anymore, I pulled out my stiff erection; the tip was dark red, even a slight breeze caused me to tighten the grip while sliding my hand up and down. She looks over, distracted by my movement until she looks at me and I wink, causing her to arch her back as she tweaks her nipple again.

I continue to torture her, "Now, where was I? Yes, then I pick you up and toss you on the bed. You giggle in anticipation when I kiss your toes to your ankles and I make my way up. I feed off your moans and gasps..."

She gasps on cue, her arm moving quicker than before while the other continues to grope her breasts.

"Colin..."

Please call me Daniel. I'm begging her in my head.

I wanted to tell her everything, make her understand, and then order her to cum while whispering my name, my real name. Every day I put up this deception the more I realize she deserves the truth. She deserves better, she deserves Daniel.

"Stop…now." She looked stunned when I commanded her. Her lips formed into a pout. "Show me both hands. Keep them where I can see them."

I can see she wanted to say something but I kept the emotion off my face so she knew this was serious and if she didn't do what she was told she would be punished even worse.

"I know you're learning but you didn't call me Daddy and you need to learn that it comes with consequences. Were you close?"

She nodded furiously.

"Use your words."

She shudders, "Ye-yes, daddy. So close."

"Next time you won't be able to cum. For a whole 24 hours. Do you understand?"

She nods feverishly, hoping I would allow her to continue. I would but when I was ready to watch her fall apart. I hold off for another minute until my lips turn upward into a smirk.

"Touch yourself as if my strong hands are caressing every inch of you, tease your sensitive nipples while you imagine me diving into your sweetness. Your fingers run through my hair as you pull, pull harder, baby. I want you to cause a little pain with my pleasure until I make my way to those soft lips. I've fantasized about them wrapped around my dick, gagging all over me. Oh, baby…you're going to make me cum down your naughty little throat if you keep going like that. Tell me what you want."

I lick my palm and tighten my grip further to simulate her tight, wet pussy. Her purring brings me out of my fantasies.

"I want to taste you, Daddy. Do it. I love when you stare down at me, when I'm on my knees for you, as I twist my hands around what I can't deep throat, creating that friction that makes your balls tighten. You groan to the sounds I make giving you a sloppy blow job. Ooh, your kitten is making such a mess…"

I didn't realize the tables had turned until I indeed felt it coming like a freight train.

Well played, but I want to see her unravel first.

"But then I bend you over the bed and give you a few licks. You scream my name when I slam into you repeatedly, begging me not to stop. I can feel your walls tightening…let go, kitten, just let go."

I look over to see her squirming. Her movements became fast, yet sloppy, as she was trying to find that magical combination. I noticed my breathing had labored to match hers.

"Daddy… please, I need to, can I cum?" My dominant side was pleased with how obedient she wanted to be, but I wanted to make sure she knew I was serious about punishments

"No."

She choked on her breath, looking to me for an explanation. I didn't owe her one.

I can see the tears welling in her eyes, I knew her pussy was pulsing, throbbing, screaming for that release. She closes her legs to dull the throbbing.

"Keep them open!" She reluctantly obeys. "Just remember at any time after you disobey, I can keep you from pleasure, multiple times. You need to learn; do I make myself clear?" My tone is harsher than usual, but she'll learn how serious her mistakes can be.

"Yes daddy, I'm sorry."

Her admittance makes me rock hard. Fuck! I enjoy seeing her teetering on the edge but now I'm ready to see her downfall.

"Be a good girl and cum for me, kitten."

She resumes punishing herself with my approval. I watch her work herself up until she arches her back. I imagine my lips kissing her all over, concentrating on those perky nipples, squeezing them while her orgasm washes over her, her walls tightening around me. Massaging her clit as her legs wrapped around me to stop the shaking. She exhales loudly, bringing me back to the present and the satisfied look in her eyes. "Oh... daddy, that was amazing, thank you."

I rub my hand up and down my chest. "Now, finish daddy off with that sexy voice of yours."

I get comfortable in bed, letting my hand slip under the waistband of my pajamas. She doesn't even ease into it, she starts by moaning 'Daddy' so heavenly, telling me how she can't wait to wrap herself around me, wanting my strong hand around her throat while she rides my dick. The thought of her riding me until she owned me would have worked, but she decided to up the ante by demonstrating how with her body pillow.

"Just imagine it's you underneath me as I rock back and forth, up and down. You feel how wet you make me then you smack me hard." She demonstrates by giving herself a good, hard lick making her ass jiggle as she continues to verbally taunt me, "The friction causes me to go faster...and faster, up and down...riding you harder and harder..."

"Fuck baby, shit!" I think I may have blacked out for a second. I don't think I've ever cum that hard and her explicit fantasy can undoubtedly take credit as she hops off the pillow that now bears her scent as she sits back like little Miss Innocent while I try to calm down from feeling like I came like a fire hose.

"Wow." That's all she said as she went back to the box of chocolates, curious to know what was in the middle. I tilt my head to the side to see her smile.

"Thank you for the flowers. The girls were swooning over them. Oh, they also want to say sorry for what you heard. It was meant to be a joke to get me to go."

"No need to explain; I overreacted."

"No, you didn't. Look, I like you, a lot and I want to know everything about you; it's what people do when they see something beyond the casual. I'm serious about us. Is that how you feel?"

I swallowed hard, hoping she didn't notice. She was everything Daniel needed and more, but she didn't know him; she only knew Colin, a fake, a liar, a shell of a man. He wasn't worthy of her.

I looked up and realized the heartbreak on her face, she noticed my silence.

"I…"

Then my phone buzzed with a tone I had only heard once before. It sounded like an amber alert but slightly different. I grabbed it before I could look back at her. There was a red banner across the message that read: CRITICAL. Location: Brooklyn, NY. Flight in two hours, job starts immediately upon arrival. Target: Antonio Manelli, crime boss of the Corsican mafia. Manifest coming in next message. Bounty: $500K.

My eyes widened when I realized I had to leave now to get to the airport.

I look over and she's already shaking her head with tears in her eyes. I hadn't answered and I interrupted us to check my phone.

"I'm sorry, kitten."

"Don't! Call me that. Just when I thought I was getting close, that we had made up, you're running the other way! You said you'd open up! What is so important that you can't even answer my question?"

"It's not like that, pussy cat." Her eyes narrowed further, not a good time for pet names. "I need to take this; it's a priority one. My flight is in less than two hours. I have to head to the airport right now or I'll miss my flight. I've recently been thinking about re…"

She holds her hand up, interrupting me. "So, it's more important than building up our relationship? I thought we were okay! Do you know what bothers me the most about your precious little 'job'? It's the fact that you don't trust me enough to tell me what exactly it is that you do?

The simplest bit of fucking information! Am I asking for too much?!"

Her arms are flailing around, she's so flustered and upset with me. She snaps her fingers and brings me back to her attention with a loud, disappointing sigh as she continues, "We're not even on the same wavelength and it breaks my heart. I'm dying to be with you, to have you hold me, touch me, every fiber screaming to have you claim me. I trusted you enough to try this most intimate curiosity again because I felt comfortable with you! You were supposed to be good for me, the one who took care of me, but you're not and you haven't! You're the worst! You're a... a bad daddy!"

The way she spat it out with so much anger and hatred made me flinch. I never wanted to be batched in with the other men who treated her so poorly, I was supposed to be her saving grace. I didn't know if anything I said could make her understand.

"Emmy, please. I've gone over this. It's for your own good that you don't know."

As I'm trying to calm her, I notice a binocular icon I do recognize; they are tracking me. With priority ones, they monitor us from the moment we receive the notification until we confirm the kill. I didn't need them to be involved in this conversation or this part of my life even if they don't monitor our video chat normally. This was different, this was a priority one, the rules no longer applied.

"You're going to have to trust me. I really have to go, please don't be mad."

I shut my computer, quickly threw everything in my bags, and got dressed.

I am dealing with a major shit storm when I log back on.

I'm not stupid, well, that may have been the dumbest thing I've done relationship-wise, but I can't think about that now.

I wanted to tell her that I am considering retiring and that this bounty would go towards that so we could live comfortably.

Yes, WE.

There was no doubt in my mind, even though we hadn't verbally said it, she was my girl, and I was hers. I would fix it when I got back, and I would notify my agency to end my contract.

Then I would introduce her to Daniel, the man who fell for her.

Emmy

"Don't you dare hang up, Colin?!...THAT SON OF A BITCH!" I scream as I stare at my profile page, signaling he hung up on me. All my welled-up tears fell in anger, but I wasn't crying; I was seething.

I threw on my robe and paced the length of my room, pulling at my hair. I didn't know what to do. I didn't know whether to laugh, scream, or throw my laptop. I angrily gathered the rose petals.

I suddenly felt dirty, like some cheap whore he paid an hour for, used me, got what he needed, and left without leaving money on the nightstand. The flowers, chocolate, and champagne were merely payoffs. I tossed everything in the garbage, I didn't want any reminder of this night, but the memories of his deep voice penetrated my mind as he coaxed me beyond my pleasure threshold. His words cause a dual reaction of pleasure and pain. I wish I could shut my brain off.

I never felt so empty. I storm into my bathroom and turn the shower on to the hottest temperature I could tolerate to scrub him off me even though he hadn't actually touched me. At the same time, I was washing down my feelings, the pain and hurt, the unknown...why was I putting up with this?!

You know why, you just won't admit it.

I cried my eyes out, let my emotions come tumbling forward, and found myself flopped down on my shower floor. I knew the answer, but my thoughts were right, I really didn't want to admit it. All I knew about Colin was what was on his profile and the little he's told me.

What was I going to do?

Colin

I almost missed my flight because all I could focus on was the heartbreak on her face and my actions. Let's face it, I was a coward and a liar.

I was on my way to the gate when they called my name for the last boarding call. I had to run down the terminal to catch my red-eye flight to New York City.

You're a bad daddy! Bad...daddy...a bad daddy.

Those words hurt every time they cycled through my head, it was self-punishment and I deserved it.

As soon as I sat in my first-class seat, I forced myself to read the downloaded manifest on Manelli. Antonio Manelli, Corsican Mafia King and public enemy #1 when it came to our agency. He ambushed and killed one of our agents. The bastard broadcasted it all over the net to prove he was invincible, that no one could get close without him finding out and making an example out of them.

He killed Pluto two years ago and then went into hiding, we've been putting out feelers for him ever since. He knew we would retaliate if we found him. I wanted his balls on a silver platter for what he did!

On the video, Pluto was bloody, bruised, almost unrecognizable in his final moments with his hands and feet tied individually to two posts, stretching him out mere inches from the ground.

Manelli enters from the left, "You sent an assassin to kill me?! Who sent you? Was it the Fratelli clan, the Morrisons? Wasted money because here I stand but your little mercenary will be a show and tell of what happens when you try to mess with me or my family, especially my son, the NEW King of Miami!"

He strides over to Pluto, slapping him in the head. You could see all the damage inflicted, probably for hours, maybe even days. From the black eye to the lumps from blunt force trauma, they probably beat him to get answers like who he worked for or who sent him but obviously he didn't say a word. His shirt was sliced in several places, indicating multiple stab wounds. He was already dying a slow death.

"But, in case you're stupid enough to make another attempt, know your fate will be exactly like his." Then he exited from screen view, and something was thrown on Pluto as he tried to squirm to avoid the huge amount of liquid hitting him but to no avail. He's screaming through the gag, and I could distinctly hear one word: FIRE

Then something hits his chest, and, in a flash, he is engulfed in flames. Watching, it felt like hours but was less than a minute due to the extensive amount of what I assume was gasoline or some accelerant. He was writhing and screaming until there was no movement and silence. He died a cruel public death, and I was going to make sure Manelli paid with every drop of his blood. He sealed his fate when he took one of our own.

Emmy

Last night was a living nightmare. I barely slept because I was battling on the inside. I wanted Colin but the secrecy and only giving me the bare minimum was unacceptable. What was I supposed to build our foundation on? Hopes and fucking dreams?

Well, screw that!

If he wasn't going to tell me, then I was going to find out on my own!

After three hours of relentless searching, I couldn't find a footprint about his past or present…not even a breadcrumb, it's like he didn't exist!

Is that what it all comes down to? That he wasn't who he said he was and had lied to me? What else could it be? The fact that he thinks I'm stupid and I would be okay with what little info he gave me pisses me off to no end. There are limits to my submissiveness and willful ignorance is not one of them. I want to let him know what I really think but he had his "priority one assignment" or whatever the hell that meant.

I let off steam in the gym, but it did not dull my rage. All the men who usually talk or flirt with me knew not to approach me today; I'm sure my resting bitch face was obvious or perhaps my screeching while hitting the punching bag was a big indicator to back off. I leave covered in sweat and bathed in frustration.

When I put the keys in the door of our condo, Carla and Tawny are walking out. It looks like they finished their daily yoga session not too long ago since they were in their sports bras and leggings. Now that I think about it, I should have ended my gym session with a bit of calming yoga, but I wanted to stew in my anger.

"Hey, Em, we're going to our favorite wrap place. You want your usu…" Tawny stopped when she saw my face. "Don't worry about it; we'll bring you back something. Go take care of it."

I peel off my clothes and pace my bathroom in a towel. I couldn't believe I fell for that salesperson bit or maybe I wanted my dream man and was willing to overlook the glaring red flags.

"He has to be dealing drugs, or maybe he's in the mob, they're very tight-lipped and wear suits all the time, too; or he could be a sadistic psycho killer and I'll be taken down as his accomplice!"

Ok, so some of those are far-fetched but my brain was coming up with all the possibilities of who Colin could be. What makes it worse is that I was falling for the part of him he wanted me to see, but why? Was I not good enough to know the real Colin? If that was even who he said he was. It's like I was being catfished and the big reveal in all of this was life-altering.

Colin

That smug son of a bitch was going to die; this was retribution, this was personal.

As I'm filling the magazine clips with rounds, there's a quick knock at my door.

No one knows I'm here except the agency. Is it possible they got the jump on me?

I take one gun and affix the suppressor. I look and see no one through the peephole. I take a deep breath and open the door quickly, raise my gun and... nothing.

I look down the hallway and see no one. I lowered the gun and walked back into my room when I heard a squeak. I quickly turn with my gun raised to see Hermes and Ares in my room and the balcony window open.

How the fuck did they knock at my door?!

Hermes kissed the tip of my gun and I dropped it.

"Fucking hell, I almost blew your goddamn face off!"

"You wish, buddy, look down." He had his sawed-off double-barrel shotgun pointed at my abdomen.

"Shit."

"You're getting slow in your old age, Zeus. Time for me to take the reins of the group, ehh?" He laughs, causing Ares to chuckle along with him, but I'm not laughing, because he's right.

Their faces fall and Hermes shakes his head in disbelief, "Are you...no way, man...you? I never thought I'd see the day you even think about it." He rubbed his hand down his ginger beard as he sat in a chair and eyed me.

I sat on the bed, putting my gun next to its brother as I ran my hands through my hair. "It's been a long time coming."

Ares sat at the kitchen island, his quiver leaning against the counter slightly as he tried to read me as well.

"Let's not muddy our minds with that right now, are you guys here to help take out Manelli?"

"Are you kidding, I've been waiting on this assignment for two years and the bounty is $500K each. We don't have to split a half mil. His head is worth almost two million dollars. Let's talk strategy; I want that bastard squealing like a pig before we gut him. Pluto deserves retribution for the way that bastard killed him."

Ares laid the quiver down, "What about his son?"

Hermes threw up his hands, "Fuck him, I'll gladly bathe in his blood when I separate his upper body from his lower. First, let's cut the head off the organization before we deal with his demon seed. Spare no one."

Hermes had that sadistic grin. He loved his job a little too much. When choosing our weapons, he made it a goal to choose the one that could cause the most bodily damage with little effort. He was one ruthless fucker.

I stand up to put the twins in my shoulder holster, "Okay, let's come up with the plan and a backup. We can't take anything to chance; we know he will have no problem executing one of us if caught. I don't know about you, but I've got a good reason to come back."

Emmy

Kayla rushes into my room, "Emmy, I don't have anything to wear for my date tonight! Can I please borrow something? I want to look special for him. It's our two-month anniversary!"

She couldn't stop smiling if she wanted to. Whoever this guy is, she is smitten. She and her last sugar daddy, Edgar, had parted ways when he told her he wanted her to find true happiness. He knew he was there just to finance her. She said she wasn't interested in him in that way. He said he understood and gave her a substantial final amount to keep up with our bills for a while.

Edgar was the quintessential true southern gentleman when it came to Kayla and us. He liked to show us off and take us to the Green Room where we would dine like the rich. He said he was lucky to know such pretty ladies at his age. He was 62, I think, and had retired early from being a stockbroker. To be honest he looked great for his age, not a day over 45. Definitely could be mistaken for someone's dad or a young grandfather.

Then not too long after their separation, Kayla deleted her page. She had met some mystery man and she said he wanted her off the site and all to himself. Which sounded sweet and a little possessive at the same time, but it was her life.

He always sent a car to pick her up and we wouldn't see her until the following day or afternoon. And let's say she had that thoroughly fucked look.

I wave my hand towards my closet, "Sure, go ahead. Grab the long-sleeved, ruched emerald, green mini dress, it'll look amazing against your skin tone, and your chunky black heels. I see a nude lip and a bold smokey eye with green in it."

She emerges from my closet with the dress. "You always know what to put together. Thank you, thank you, thank you!" She squeals as she closes my door.

I focus back on my finger hovering dangerously close to the enter key, a motion that would delete my profile from the site.

You're the worst! You're a… a bad daddy!

I took it too far when I screamed that to his face. I saw him flinch, but I was just so hurt, I wanted to hurt him, and I had. The worst thing you could ever tell any daddy. As a daddy he was perfect, loving, nurturing, and caring.

The enraged me wants to delete my page and temporarily find someone to satisfy my craving to be fucked into oblivion, but the emotional me wants answers and to fix it and stay, to finally be wrapped up in the comforting arms of my daddy.

But *who* was it I was trying to stay with really?

Colin

We returned to my hotel covered in Manelli's blood, his entourage, and every single person who made the decision to associate themselves with him.

Thankfully I was wearing a trench coat to cover the blood splatter on my clothes. I was able to wipe most of it off my face to not look like I walked through a slaughterhouse. We used my room key to unlock the rear exit door and find the nearest elevator. I'll have the agency wipe the footage of us entering from the security cameras before anyone sees three blood-soaked men entering the hotel.

Hermes, of course, was wearing the blood on his face like a badge of honor. We viciously killed Antonio Manelli in honor of our brother Pluto.

When we entered my room, I started my routine while confirming the assignment was complete and requesting the security cam footage be wiped. We sent video and photos back to the agency and our vendetta was complete. Revenge never tasted so sweet.

Hermes takes paper towels and wets them to wipe off his face. Ares looked as clean as when he came here but his quiver was empty, he did as much damage as Hermes but from a distance. I've never seen an arrow pierce a man's eye and the momentum push pieces of his brain through the exit wound. I'm sure it will haunt my nightmares.

"Alright, quit pissing off, what's the retirement deal? Have you told the agency?"

"No, not yet. It's been a thought for the past few months or so. I can't do this forever, I'm no spring chicken."

Ares wags his finger; he had been silently analyzing me. "You are the best of the best despite your age. This isn't about age; this is about a woman. I know the signs; you forget I've studied body language."

Ares smirked confidently as he looked at me and I folded, "Fine, you're right. She's absolutely everything I could ever want. It was all going great until..." I groan internally as it all flashes in my head again.

Hermes breaks my attention when he swirls his scotch. "Uh oh, there it is, what did you do?"

"We were video chatting when I took this assignment, and she went off about not knowing what I do and I told her I couldn't then I... I hung up on her. To catch my flight!" I tried to justify my actions, but I'm met with dual groans. I cringed to know that it sounded as bad, if not worse, as the action itself.

"What's worse is she called me a bad daddy." I knew I would have to explain but I need some insight into what to do to fix it.

"Maybe I am, I'm more than twice her age, why would she want to be tethered to some old man?"

See, as easy as that, your confidence can disappear. I felt like complete and utter shit.

"No sugar coating it, mate, you definitely fucked up. You may retire and come back to no one. Have you spoken to her since? Listen, what you are into is none of our business and we don't judge, hell, I've been a daddy before, but she was a super brat, the kind you wouldn't mind putting a hit on." He chuckles while nudging my shoulder, "but this lass seems like the one for you, but you have got to right this very bad wrong."

Ares stands up and gathers his quiver, "What Hermes said is correct. But trust me, you got to let her cool off, she is about as hot as lava, and she won't give a damn about anything you have to say. Especially after what she said to you, which, don't take it to heart, I'm sure she said it out of anger and to hurt you. You need to take that time and think about the entire situation. You need to get out of here and find a place to sort this out and DO NOT go to where she is. I'll tell the agency you're utilizing your comp time for at least 96 hours."

"Five days?! I'm not sure I can..."

Hermes pulls out a celebratory cigar, searching his pockets for his lighter. "Listen to us, Zeus, you need to really think this out and you won't be able to if you keep taking assignments. You can't avoid this. We will cover for you, we did learn from the best, you know." He winks when he says that last part and then lights his cigar, "and really think about what's best for her, not just what you want. We got to go, book a flight tonight and get out of here. Once news of Manelli's brutal assassination hits the streets they'll be combing the city."

I could only agree. They exit out of the balcony leaving me with their advice and my thoughts. I'm a Class A assassin and I'm having my heart squeezed by a girl who can't even rent a car.

I wonder what she's doing.
How much damage did I cause?
Did I make her cry?

I started to feel the guilt burning in the pit of my stomach, telling me I needed to apologize for being so cold. Shame that dug up who I really was and threw it in my face, the ugly reminder that I'm not the wonderful man she thinks I am. It reminds me of all the times I failed her by perpetuating myself as Colin. Including now.

Sick of my own thoughts, I called the airline and booked a red-eye flight.

No matter what I do I couldn't kill these feelings and I needed to sort it out.

Emmy

It's been five days and I have not heard a peep from Colin.

I was concentrating on my continued studies. Nothing was going to get in the way of my dreams, not even some... man. But he wasn't some man, he was my daddy.

Was, Ember, was!

Eventually, I found myself on the site, not even reading the messages, comments, or notes, deleting them if they weren't from him. It was a form of self-inflicted torture. I should delete it and him out of my life and move on. I have no need to be on this site after him anyway. I just had it because my roommates did, I was the only one not really using it for its intended purpose.

I did find myself on Naughtyfet down a wormhole of information. So many articles from experienced doms and their subs. Along with some general similarities among all of them. They all stressed that you make it work for you. No one can come into your relationship and say what's wrong. And, as a newbie, it comforted me that hopefully, I was doing well as his sub-in-training.

But back to reality, after my failed background search on him, I'm even more sure he wasn't who he said he was.

Just thinking about it pisses me off all over again! I scream into my pillow as the girls walk in. I have spent most of my time holed up here since that horrible night. I knew eventually they'd send in a search party.

Millicent slams my books shut and Carla takes my laptop, closes it, and puts it on my dresser.

"Enough, Em. You won't tell us what happened between you and Colin, but you have been sulking and avoiding public appearances even in your own house. We're not going to let you keep doing this, period. Friday, we are going out to celebrate Kayla's birthday and you are going to go if I have to kidnap you and shove liquor down your throat!"

"Sheesh!" I hold my hands up, "You're right; no need to threaten me. I wouldn't miss celebrating Kayla's 21st birthday for anything in the world! I got to get out of this funk anyway. Kayla, we're going to get you so drunk!"

She shakes her head, "Oh no...we are going to Sinner's nightclub, Jimmy owns it, and he's going to meet me there. I can't be sloppy drunk. I need to be super sexy when my man walks in and sees me! OW!" She shakes her hips and uses my bedpost as a stripper pole causing me to laugh to tears. One of those laughs that make you forget about all your cares. Kayla plops down beside me, "I'm so glad I don't have to flirt and hang out with old men anymore. Jimmy's going to take care of me now." We egg her on and this lifts my spirits, just me and my girls. I was looking forward to Friday. I needed to let loose and throw caution to the wind.

Colin

I spent five days home in St. Louis, but I didn't tell Vincent this time. I had to figure it all out and his sophomoric antics were not what I needed right now.

I found myself visiting a place I hadn't been to in a while, my parent's graves. They were perched up on a hill with a beautiful view when the sunset. I paid a pretty penny for that spot to make sure they were together. My father had died of a heart attack on the job and not a week later did my mom die from a weak heart, but we all knew she died from a broken heart. I always imagined that my dad was waiting for her at the pearly gates to welcome her home, together forever.

When my mother was alive, she would impart wisdom about life and what she wanted for her only son. Her hopes for me were different from that of my three sisters, who were all married with families, and then there was me. She said I'd eventually marry but she saw a wandering spirit that I needed to take care of first. She said don't worry about how old you are when you marry, worry about loving her with your entire heart and she will give you everything you could ever need.

That was Emmy.

I sat between their graves after I did some cleaning up, laying fresh flowers on mom's grave and a box of cigars for dad. He loved to enjoy one after a long day managing the construction site.

It was a partly sunny day, and the clouds were passing by slowly. I talked as if they were listening, spilling everything that was on my heart. I felt like my mom was whispering her thoughts in the gentle breeze that surrounded me. She came down from heaven to tell her little boy what was most important in life, and she was right. After three hours, I felt like I had a course of action.

As I was heading back to my hotel, I had gotten an assignment notification; guess it was back to work and I was flying to…

Perfect timing.

"Oh, I'm coming for you, kitten."

Emmy

Tonight, was Kayla's 21st birthday celebration and I was looking to dance my cares away. I was going to document every dirty detail of the night on Sweetsugar, I even edited my byline: *Liars need not apply.* And then tomorrow, I will delete it, no hesitation this time.

Ooh, I am smoking hot! I look over my strapless yellow bandage dress and white strappy heels. I love how it pops against my warm skin and is even better when I've had some time in the sun.

It's probably illegal to wear something this scandalous, but I am, to piss off Colin, or whatever his name is and there's nothing he can do about it. Hell, for all I know, he's probably clear across the country and moved on to some other girl to take care of.

Another princess.

He…he didn't need me anymore.

Doesn't matter. I want nothing more to do with him; in fact, whatever this was, is over. I didn't even know who he was and our foundation was already flawed…and yet still…

Kayla knocks me out of my thoughts when she struts in wearing a scandalously sheer red lace dress and black pumps. "Emmy, do you think this is okay?"

I thought I was half-naked. Obviously, she was trying to show off for her new man. Apparently, he was a successful businessman in Miami, but we all know that's code for a crime boss or drug lord.

"Wow, Kay, you look amazing!"

"I really want to look nice for Jimmy, this is the first public appearance I'll have with him and I want to turn heads. I want all the girls to know that Jimmy is mine!"

I spin her around, "Well, that'll be obvious! You are smoking hot girl!" She squealed in excitement. Then, she gives me a once-over, "Holy shit Emmy, who are you trying to bag?"

"Any man who wants it tonight!" I said it so nonchalantly while fixing my dress, I realized it sounded super harsh and I saw her flinch.

"But...what about Colin?" Her voice softened and I saw the concern, but I'm not here for it.

"Colin who?" I left it at that as I went into my bathroom to set my beach waves and run my finger across my wine-stained lips. I turn to see the back of my dress, it's barely legal. I walk towards her, grabbing my clutch, then I link our arms, "Let's go, sweet meat!"

I ignored the pain in my heart. I felt like I was betraying him, but he hurt me. I don't need this right now. Time to focus on the birthday girl!

I'm brought out of my thoughts by the honking of a car; it must be the limo. I shake my head and get back into party girl mode and head outside. What I thought was supposed to be a classic limo turned out to be a sleek, black, Escalade party bus. The driver held the passenger door open; we were bombarded by strobe lights and loud music. Kayla was elated! She danced her way right into the bus and we followed. She pops up from the roof as we climb in. "See! I told you Jimmy would take good care of me! Who knows, maybe he'll move me in with him."

By the time I got in, Carla was pouring shots of Bacardi 151. "To the birthday girl and her man providing the ultimate VIP experience. To the night!" We all repeat and slam the shots down. Carla pours again and promises this is the last one, too many and we won't even make it to the club.

We arrive and are quickly escorted inside to the platinum VIP area with our matching silver wristbands. Our section was empty, her beau hadn't made it yet and I was curious to meet him. She hadn't told us much because she said she wanted to make sure it was solid and not a fling. I was starting to believe that Kayla grew out of her sugar baby phase and was looking for something more substantial.

A bit later

"Hey ma, in the sexy yellow dress, let me buy you a drink, whatever you want, top-shelf!" I hear some guy yell over the music as we head back to VIP from the dance floor. I saunter a bit sexier to tease. Being able to buy top-shelf liquor wasn't enticing to me, I can usually get my drinks free anyway because Dominic, my ex, was the manager here. He was a sinfully gorgeous Puerto Rican man with deep green eyes and a tongue that could...well, let's not talk about that. It could give a girl flashbacks and hot flashes. He was way too vain for his own good.

He could have any girl he wanted, and that cocky bastard did during our entire relationship; he couldn't stay monogamous if a gun was pointed at his dick, ready to blow off his prized possession.

Rather than run the risk of the inevitable visit to the clinic, I left him quickly. He still tries repeatedly to come back, saying I was the best girl he's ever had.

Tuh, I knew that.

He realized way too late, but I use his incessant begging to my advantage by hooking a VIP area for me and my girls. He thinks it increases his chances of getting back into my pants.

I stood against the rail, ignoring all the guys trying to get my attention. They were the usual college guys. You know hot, horny, and wouldn't last longer than the time to toast a pop tart.

I was looking for the older gentlemen who usually reserve a VIP spot, sit back, and observe their surroundings smoking cigars while sipping on $300 bottles of scotch or cognac. Their prey would come to them or entice them from the dance floor. They would make a simple hand gesture to reel them in. That gesture would hold so much dominance, it drives a submissive crazy.

I wonder if he drinks or smokes? He would look so sexy smoking a cigar.

Would he come to a place like this? Use his dominance to draw me to him and seduce me.

I would bend to his will, easy.

Stop it, Emmy; we're moving on!

I feel a pair of hands slide around my waist before pulling me against them. I smell his subtle woodsy cologne. I know that scent all too well. I confirm what I know by looking down and seeing his Puerto Rico flag and his mother's name tattooed on his forearm.

"Hi, Dom." I said flatly.

"Fuck *bella*, you look sexy as hell. Tell me this is all for me?" He growled in my ear then kissed it.

I look back and laugh, "You wish." He licks his lips while eyeing me up and down. It used to make me weak in the knees but since Colin…I internally curse myself.

How many times do I got to say it? It's over. You need to find a new Daddy.

"Dom, get me a Cosmo, will ya? Thanks, doll face." He hates those super sweet pet names which is why I used it as a repellent. I lean forward and shift my weight as I catch him staring before he disappears into the crowd. Tawny dances against me to take my mind off everything.

Unfortunately, Dom comes back with my drink. Not deterred by the sappy pet name, his hands once again slide around my waist as he kisses my shoulder heading towards the sweet spot on my neck. He knows how that affects me, but I am in no mood.

"Dom, stop. I told you, I'm not interested. Not now, not ever."

"But *mami*, that dress says something different. It says you're looking for trouble and here I am. Come on, we had good times. I always had you writhing under me, didn't I?"

I hate to admit it but he's right. Unfortunately, he was community dick, like a revolving door. Probably fucked half this crowd judging by all the nasty looks I was getting with him all over me. Don't worry; I have no intention of more than what's going on right now.

"Look, I'm only here to piss off my boyfriend, nothing more." I attempt to take a selfie, but Dom weasels his way into it. I set it as my new profile pic; that should stir the pot a bit because he'll get a notification when it uploads. If we were on the straight and narrow this picture would most definitely have gotten me punished for being a bad girl. Just the thought of his big hands caressing my ass before it connected hard and I yelped before I moaned. Fuck, I was getting so wet at the thought.

"Boyfriend? You know he'll never be like me. Where is he? I wouldn't let you out of my sight dressed like that. Do I know him?"

His rambling cockiness is really irritating.

"What's with all the personal questions? It's truly none of your business."

Millicent suddenly grabs me and drags me to the bar. "Don't let him get to you, let's have a good time!" I'm glad she calmed me down, my inner bitch was surfacing, and I was about to hand him his balls. My anger hadn't entirely dissipated from Colin and Dom was about to feel my fist.

Even though I'm mad, I miss him, I do. I miss being cared for and doted on, I miss being called his princess or his kitten. I don't feel right being here with so much unresolved between us.

The girls all line up in front of our personal bartender. He was topless and quite buff, he flirted with all of us, but he was fond of Milli. I ordered myself a dirty little virgin and dropped a bill in his tip jar.

Then both club doors open and a guy in a white suit and pink button-up strolls through as the crowd moves out of his way. Kayla squeals, "That's him, that's my Jimmy!" I look back and watch as he makes his rounds through the club; undoubtedly, he'll end up here with her.

He reminded me of Dominic with that air of arrogance that he was untouchable. I guess he was, he owned this place and in Miami, that gave you status. I wondered what other dealings was he involved in?

Once he was done *"schmoozing,"* he approached Kayla, who was rocking side to side with her hands behind her, pretending to be an innocent doll in a slutty dress.

"Mi Bella…" He kisses her cheek and she blushes.

"Hola Papi, I missed you." (hi daddy) She takes his hand in both of hers as she leaned against him.

"And you, too, Princess. *Feliz cumpleaños."* (happy birthday)

He kisses her hand and she's grinning from ear to ear. *"Gracias."* (thank you)

He turns towards the rest of us, "Why don't you introduce me to your lovely friends. Ladies…"

"Sure, this is Millicent, Carla, Tawny, and Ember. This is Jimmy." We all nod in acknowledgment.

"Nice to meet you, Millicent, Carla, Tawny, and… Ember." He lingered on my name and his leering was a little uncomfortable, but I smiled as Kayla danced against him and his attention was back on her. Maybe I was seeing things. Watching them dance made me think about Colin.

Okay, everything did; I was so screwed.

Colin

I take in the view of the lively Miami skyline, spotlights signaling where the best parties were but for a hefty price. I was pacing the patio while I was waiting for a report. This wasn't just any standard report. I had done the one thing I always do with any potential person from the beginning, but I hadn't even thought about it for Emmy until I was in my current bind.

I ran a background check on her.

I honestly had no rhyme or reason to except that if I could potentially spend my life with her, I needed to be sure she was who she says she was.

The irony, huh?

Maybe I wanted to justify my lying by bringing up any of her indiscretions. I needed to know everything about her.

My phone buzzes and there's her report.

"Ember Calynn Peters," Such a beautiful name, "interesting, she's not 18 she's 22. She lied about her age to seem...younger? I wonder why? She's also not a student but a graduate of the University of Miami. Summa cum laude, I'm not surprised, she's the brains between us.

I see that a few of her exes reside in town, a couple graduated the same year she did, and one is a promoter for a club in the party district. Of course, I look him up and he looks like the typical arrogant punk only looking to find someone for the night. I skim the rest of the report and find nothing outstanding other than her lying about her age and school status.

I hear a ping from my laptop, a notification from Sweetsugar. It can only be about Emmy; I only subscribed to her updates. I opened it and saw she added a new profile picture. I click and see her, scantily clad and dolled up, next to some guy hugged up on her and I realize it's her ex. She captioned it, "A sexy siren ready for a night of reckless abandonment. Oh, and Dominic. *Eye roll* haha!"

Sounds like he's more of an annoyance than interest, that makes me feel better, I guess, but I can't risk someone taking her from me. I click out of the picture and it takes me back to her profile, where I noticed a change to her byline.

"Liars need not apply."

Wow.

She was acting out after I abandoned our conversation, after making up, ignored her for an assignment then hung up and ghosted her. I literally had no one to blame but myself, but I wasn't going to give up without a fight. She will listen to what I have to say. I hop in the shower, my mind fucked from my kitten's picture and the byline, this is far from over.

I had to remember that I was here on a recon mission. Jimmy Gregarno had made quite a name for himself in the short time he moved his business to the greater Miami district. He was gaining power almost instantly by offering a better product than his competition, causing a power shift. A few of those competitors who didn't willingly side with Jimmy seemed to have disappeared. Additionally, to the disappearance of his rivals, there was intel he was running some dark operation, but info was little to non-existent. The only ones that knew the details were Jimmy and his closest men. Finding out exactly what it was is my assignment.

I had another hour before I would walk into the club as another patron celebrating the weekend to get eyes on Jimmy. I was able to crack the security cams for the club; it was Fisher-Price level. I spotted Emmy and some guy grinding against her in the VIP section.

Who the fuck is he?!

I zoom in. She nudges him and smiles, a drink in her hand. He is way too close and comfortable to be some random stranger. Matter of fact, he looks like the ex from the newly added profile picture. By the way he was dancing and touching her, watching her curves brush against him, it was clear he wanted to reclaim her. And she was playfully pushing him away but not in a serious manner. Judging by her dress, she was looking to get into a whole lot of trouble. Little did she know she was going to get it...from me. I'll spank her ass until it's as red as a stop sign and she's dripping wet with arousal. I'll keep her on edge until she's begging me to cum. I couldn't wait to get my hands on my disobedient little pussy cat.

I slip on my suit jacket and head out to Sinners.

As much as I am aroused, I'm also ticked off. I don't understand?! Was she trying to rile me up on purpose? Because she succeeded. This was a bit of bratty behavior, but it wasn't as off-putting as other girls and it wasn't to the level of super brat, I had caused her to act out.

I realized that if some drunk punk wanted to be stupid and pick a fight with me at the club, I would probably break his fingers and compound fracture his arm within the blink of an eye. I was in no mood.

I stroll up to the 2nd level of the club, giving me a bird's eye view of the entire venue. I haven't spotted Jimmy yet, so I'm observing the typical crowd filled with college kids, probably some underage, and the 25-35 crowd. I may be older, but I look like I could still fit in. I sip my bourbon while eyeing all the young women who sexily move their bodies to the beat, yet none of them compared to Emmy.

I keep my eye on her while trying to complete my mission. I take the required photos for the agency and make some notes about Jimmy's behavior and any information I could get on his secret operation. I wasn't there to kill him, but the ex with his paws all over Emmy may disappear tonight!

Emmy

The girls were in the middle of the dance floor; you'd think that's precisely where I'd want to be, getting the attention I deserved, but no, I was in our section watching them. My heart was screaming to go home, and I started to feel like I didn't want to be there. It was hard enough getting Dom to get off me, luckily some bimbo distracted him and his chances of getting laid were higher than his zero with me, so he left. I was alone in my thoughts. I felt my confidence wane and my emotions began to bubble up to the surface. Suddenly a pair of arms box me against the handrail and it's not Dom.

"*Cariño*, (sweetie) how about we take a walk to my office and I can show you a good time. You look like a screamer."

I look back to see Jimmy and I could feel him, too. I use my shoulder to break the caging to get away from him.

"Uh, no, you're Kayla's man and I have… I have a boyfriend."

He tsks as he runs his finger down my neck to my shoulder. I shudder in disgust, "That sounds like a lie… Come on, I already heard from Dominic how…feisty you are in bed. Now I want to have my own personal taste test."

Dominic, that dirty son of a bitch. I'm going to snatch his balls off the next time I see him. I stepped away and looked to see that Kayla was too caught up in the scene to look up here. I blink and he's way too close for my comfort, I can smell the liquor on his breath as he whispers, "No worries, I'll have you one way or another, whether you want to or not." I quickly scurry over to the safety of the group. It was time to go. Everything about him is wrong.

The girls whoop and holler when I join their circle. I conceal my emotions while pretending to enjoy myself when all I wanted to do was get the hell out of there.

I needed Colin.

Colin

I almost blew my cover to blow Jimmy's fucking balls off when he touched my girl! She quickly broke free, but he was persistent until she scurried to the safety of her group. I grip the glass so tight it may shatter.

I close my eyes and take a couple deep breaths to calm down. Then I saw her, there she was swaying to the beat with her girlfriends, I could see she was still disgusted. Her heart wasn't in it, she looked like she was going through the motions. I secretly hope she's wanting her daddy to rescue her.

Even though she was faking her enthusiasm, she danced as if no one was watching, but plenty of men were.

While she continued dancing, I was hailing a taxi to my hotel with all the info I got on Jimmy; this would be a multi-day surveillance which was to my advantage being in the same city as her. My cold demeanor forced her to seek attention elsewhere and she got more than enough tonight. Now I needed to make it right.

When I got settled in my room and opened the surveillance footage, she was now seated in the VIP area, a different drink in her hand as she danced in her seat. I finally text her.

C: Princess…

I watch her look at her phone then put it away.

C: Princess, I want to make this right. Talk to daddy, please.

When in doubt, beg.

E: After all this time? No, I'm busy, besides, don't you have more important things to attend to rather than wasting time with me?

Ooh, she's compounding her punishment by lying, but she wants to hurt me. I get it but I also want to punish her disrespectful mouth. Punish it with my dick, watching her try to deepthroat me in entirety but looking up with the most angelic eyes. Fuck, I can't focus...

C: I'm sorry about that, but I have good news. I'll tell you if you follow my directions.

I watch her stare at her phone and bite her lip, contemplating. Naturally, curiosity got the best of her.

E: What?

C: Watch your tone. Now, take a taxi to the Austin Bordello hotel, go to the concierge, and tell them you are a guest of Mr. Wentworth.

I saw the fear in her eyes momentarily when I corrected her. Then she gasped, bringing her phone closer to her face like she couldn't believe it, or she was intoxicated and couldn't focus. Then a smile formed as she bit her finger. One of her roommates leaned over to ask her something. She answered and judging by her hand movements, she was trying to get out of there. Finally, her roommate hugs her, and she stands, pulls down her incredibly sexy dress, and walks out of the VIP area. She got stopped a couple of times, but she shook her head adamantly and pulled away each time.

Good girl.

I felt my inner dominant growl in approval. Before she was out of the camera view, she took out her phone, probably ordering her ride. Then I got a ping on my phone.

E: You're here?!

C: Yes, kitten. I can't wait to see you.

E: Okay, daddy.

There was my sliver of hope when she called me daddy. Ooh, it does things to me and now I'm hard as concrete. I called the front desk to tell them that I was expecting a guest who would give my name and to give her a key. I even gave her a description of what Emmy looked like and what she was wearing. Hopefully, they don't disclose that bit of information or how they got it. I eagerly hop in the shower and get ready to finally have my kitten underneath me.

Emmy

I was having an okay time; I still couldn't get over Jimmy's gross proposition and all under Kayla's nose. It didn't sit well, but I tried to power through the night for the birthday girl.

I was dancing in my seat when my phone buzzed. I looked to see it was a text from Colin and quickly ignored it. Before my phone was comfortably put away, it buzzed again. I huffed to read his message, replying sharply, still agitated about the incident. He let me know he didn't care for my smart mouth but said he had a surprise for me.

The song changes and it's one of my favorites, but I can't focus as I read his instructions for me...to go to his hotel! I can't believe it, he's finally here! I bite my finger to keep from squealing. All the anger I had seemed to melt away for a moment, then it came roaring back as I remember how I've felt these past few days.

Kayla asked me what was going on because I was deep in my phone. I said I was headed home to sort something out, but I was headed to the hotel to find out who Mr. Wentworth really is.

Colin

I sit back and daydream about the time we've already spent together. The long talks about any and everything, the uncontrollable laughs, and the countless times I put a smile on her face and vice versa.

She was good for me, but I still had apprehension about this situation. She was falling for a false portrayal of myself and not the real me. Is there much of a difference between Colin and Daniel? Perhaps not, but Daniel is more vulnerable than cold and calculated Colin. Daniel's been locked away so long I'm not sure how to revert back, but I know Daniel is good for Emmy. Colin's job is a liability.

I'm brought out of my thoughts when the door beeps and opens slowly. Finally, I am in the presence of my princess. I started from her sexy high heels that screamed 'fuck me,' and I wanted to, not even giving her a chance to breathe. Her dress complimented her beautiful skin tone and accentuated her dangerous curves, I can't say I didn't ogle her voluptuous breasts.

There she was, my little submissive in training, but then I was startled out of my fantasies when she slammed the door.

Well, my hope for a sexual rendezvous was extinguished by the look on her face; it was a mixture of anger and hurt.

She saunters forward, setting her purse down.

"Well, hello... Colin. Or is that even your real name?" I heard a growl from my dominant side, he is displeased by her confrontation. He wants to punish that dirty mouth of hers, maybe tie her up until she apologizes and begs me to take her. Then Daniel reminds me of what we've done. I look at this beautiful girl who is so disappointed in the man she sees before her.

She's still screaming at me, "No, it can't be because there's nothing about you anywhere online. So, it means one of two things, you either exist and had your info wiped to cover your tracks because you're in the mafia or married, or you're not who you say you are, so which lie is it, huh?! Doesn't matter because this..." She motions between us. "is over!"

I see the angry tears collecting in her eyes, but she's too upset to let them fall. When she makes the move to leave, I grab her and slam her against the door, her arms pinned above her head. Her gaze turned lustful in her vulnerable position, chest heaving. My body heats up exponentially with her finally being in my literal grasp. Her lips are a hair away from mine as she looks through me into my soul; it's the moment I've been fantasizing about since we met.

It's our first physical kiss.

Emmy

"Get off me! Are you kidding me?!" I freed myself from his grasp and immediately shove him, releasing all my anger into it. He stumbles back, looking shocked by my reaction. Yes, I wanted that kiss, the electricity between us was so intense but I couldn't get over the fact that I was looking at a liar.

"Why? Every single day you looked me in the face and lied! I thought you were perfect...I thought you were different."

I watched him run his fingers through his hair. How I wanted to tug on it in the throes of passion right there on his bed. Hell, he could slam me on the kitchen counter and take me there. But I needed answers, the question was, would he give them to me?

He started pacing the room, fighting his demons on whether or not to justify his actions. That moment of hesitation was enough to get my answer and I was disappointed that I saw something in him.

"Wow, your silence speaks volumes right now. Great to know where I really stand with you, Colin, or whoever you are."

"Stop calling me that." He growled, annoyed I wasn't being his obedient little pet, but I didn't care.

"NO! It's who you are is it not? That's who I was introduced to and since you lied, and still won't tell me the truth, I can speak as I please. You're a liar!" I screamed the last part and then threw up my hands.

I'm so emotionally exhausted.

"For Christ's sake, I lied to keep you safe!" He exploded, "You lied about your age and about graduating college? What was the point of that, huh?"

That's cute. He thought he had a proper rebuttal.

"Keep me safe? My god, what kind of shit are you in?! Are you in the mob or mafia or something?"

I am so over him dancing around the subject, but I can't push myself to leave. Instead, I walked over to the kitchen area and sat on the barstool, shaking my head in disbelief. I put my face in my hands and sighed loudly.

Fuck my life.

Colin

She's upset and rightly so. I lied and kept things from her. It was me, what I do, who may know me, by an alias or not, and the potential for them to find those I care about and hurt me by hurting them. There's always this chance for retribution and besides my sisters, Emmy is all I had.

When she finally looked up her face was streaked with tears. I never really thought about how strongly she felt about me. So, I wrap my arm around her while she stays seated. God, she felt amazing...

"I'm sorry. You are the light in my life, but what I do is dangerous, so dangerous. I'd set the world on fire if something happened to you because of it. I swear I did it to keep you safe." I hoped that helped her understand.

She shoves me off her and it hurts. "Keep me safe? I don't even know who you are! The real you!" A nervous laugh slips her lips as she waves her hands wildly, "And how do I know I'm safe right now? You could be a killer in addition to a cold-hearted liar! The simple answer is because I trust my heart! I know you wouldn't hurt me, well physically wouldn't. A broken heart is quite a different kind of pain, isn't it?" Her voice was filled with pain but to know definitively that I broke her heart crushed me. "You want to know why I lied about my age? Because a guy I was in a relationship with told me I was too old to be on the site, he belittled me into believing I had to be younger, that I wasn't good enough as is. He messed with my confidence, only adding to my insecurities. You made me feel special! You were there for me, and now, I find out that you are a figment of my imagination. My Prince Charming doesn't exist!" She stands up abruptly, the chair scraping against the tile. She grabs her purse, wiping her face angrily. She shook her head while looking at me and it froze me in place.

"I really saw something with you. I was so hopeful, all I wanted was for you to let me in."

"Ember, sweetheart, please, let me explain."

She scoffed and rolled her eyes, "Wow, I never told you my full first name. Guess you did your own little investigation. Did you find what you're looking for...because I didn't. You don't have to worry about me anymore, I won't be your burden. Goodbye 'Colin'."

I flinched when she air quoted my name and with a final heartbroken look, she walked out my door.

Emmy

I thought he was enough for me. He was sweet, caring, and took good care of me as a daddy should, but lied to me. I still never found out what he did.

For a second, a brief moment, all I wanted was to throw the argument aside. For him to take me, to finally feel his touch, his lips all over me, his hands caressing every inch of me, spending the entire night in his arms after a year of pent-up sexual energy and cyber teasing. Now I was back at square one, even more bitter and alone.

I quietly stepped in the house, but I heard footsteps towards me after the door closed. Then I see everyone but Kayla.

"Emmy! What happened, where did you go after the club, what's wrong?"

Just a little side note, never ask what's wrong. It only makes it worse. Now I'm sobbing into Carla's arms as they walk me to my room and lay me on my bed.

"Emmy, listen very carefully to me, did someone hurt you?" Milli strokes my hair waiting for me to answer.

I shake my head, thinking, not physically but emotionally, I'm shattered.

"Do you want to talk about it?" I hear someone say, but I shake my head and cuddle a pillow wishing that this was all a bad dream. I squeeze my eyes trying to shut off my thoughts.

Then, I felt movement and I saw them all shuffled around on my bed. I had a queen, so we were all able to fit comfortably. They place their hands on my head, shoulder, and hand. I was surrounded by my sisters, it let me know they weren't going anywhere. I close my eyes to end this horrible night.

Colin

I should let this go and let her heal and move on, but I can't. I needed her and I had one last trick up my sleeve.

Total and complete honesty.

After that, it would be up to her to decide if I was worthy of an angel like her.

I paced my room before I opened my computer and logged in. She hadn't blocked me yet, but I knew she would. She wouldn't check her page tonight; I had hurt her too badly. Hopefully, she was being consoled by her friends.

I realized something by tonight's interaction, her words, her emotions...she meant much more to me than I led myself to believe. I was hurting myself, believing I was protecting her when I was causing her unnecessary pain.

I'm such a stupid, foolish idiot.

Daniel would have never done this.

She's such a good girl, so what she lied about her age? It was nothing compared to hiding my whole entire being. I have to make this right before my next assignment takes me away. It was now or never.

Killerinstinct69: Ember, I am more than sorry for lying. You're right, I owe you the truth and I want to give you the truth if you let me. I'm not sure if you ever want to hear from me again, but I want to make this right. I genuinely care about you; you mean the world to me. I will tell you anything you

want, meet me here at 8 pm. I can admit it, I need you. Please.

I hope she will give me one more shot. I really do need her.

Emmy

I woke up looking horrible, feeling worse, still in my club clothes and my makeup smeared. I was a wreck. I scrambled around the girls and took a shower to only put some loungewear on. I had no plans to be social.

By the time I emerged, the girls had scattered to their bedrooms to freshen up or go back to sleep, like Milli, our resident koala. If you're looking for her, start with the 20 blankets on her bed, she's probably in there somewhere. I wish I could sleep my frustration and sadness away.

I sit on my bed with my laptop, reluctant to even open it. I know what's there, a message from him. The typical lame 'I'm sorry' apology. I was adamant about canceling my account or blocking him, but my heart sinks when I consider it. I didn't have the heart to do either.

I took a deep breath and opened it right up to the site, I didn't even close my browser and right there was a giant red '1' on the message icon.

I clicked around, to my notifications, the dozen or so likes on my pictures, a few desperate comments, but I ignored them as I stared at that number. I didn't have to reply but he would see when I read it.

Grow up, Ember. This is serious.

I groaned at my childishness and clicked the envelope and sure enough, there was his handle in bold unread font, Killerinstinct69. Looks like he wrote it right after I left. I double-tap to open the entire message.

Killerinstinct69: Ember, I am more than sorry for lying. You're right, I owe you the truth and I want to give you the truth if you let me. I'm not sure if you ever want to hear from me again, but I want to make this right. I genuinely care about you; you mean the world to me. I will tell you anything you want, meet me here at 8 pm. I can admit it, I need you. Please.

I can't deny I want it back to the way it used to be, but it was all a lie before. I took a deep breath, like my life depended on it, and replied.

Kittenwantstoplay: You're right, Colin, I DON'T want to hear from you again.

I can't do this. I'm not sure if I ever can again.

I shut my computer angrily and decided to hang out at the pool instead of moping.

Fine, I was going to mope at the pool. I should at least have some decent scenery.

I slipped on that red thong bikini meant for him, grabbed my towel, shades, a book and walked through the house.

I was surprised when I saw a male form lying on our sofa, but he wasn't lying there, he was all over Kayla. My shuffling caused them to break up.

"Emmy! I heard about what happened after you left the club. Everyone rushed home when you didn't respond to the texts or calls to see if you were okay, but you weren't here. It put a serious damper on MY birthday night. Are you feeling any better?"

I ignored her snide remark and condescending tone, I wasn't in my right mind, and I might lash out. I shrug my shoulders, "Yeah, I decided to throw on my bikini and get some sun and forget all about him."

Jimmy sits up, wiping Kayla's lipstick off. "Hmm, man problems? I'm sure he's a fool for whatever he did, especially having a girl like you."

Jimmy eyed me up and down and it made me uncomfortable, especially because the towel was across my arm and not around my waist.

It's a house full of girls, we even sunbathed topless from time to time but now he was here a lot.

"Hello, Jimmy. Yeah, I suppose. I'll leave you guys to...whatever. Have a good day."

I couldn't make out Kayla's facial expression, but Jimmy's was very blatant and repulsive as he continued to stare at me as I walked away. I made sure to wrap my towel around my waist immediately.

He creeps me the fuck out, something about him is off and I'm not sure Kayla sees it, or she's ignoring it to be taken care of by him. Either way, I didn't want to be in the middle of any drama; I'm still reeling from my own.

I'm glad I only brought a book to get into, I was electronically disconnected, and I would keep going as long as I could. I had enough money saved up to pay for the next three months so perhaps I would spend some time looking for a part-time job.

I finally received an email update; the announcement of the kinesiology program awardees will come out in the next few weeks. My lifelong dream could come true with one phone call or email, or it could crash and burn and I'd have to start at a gym or massage parlor to get my experience while still taking classes specifically for how the body uses its muscles, bones, and ligaments to move.

After completion of the program, the top students are offered various lucrative opportunities such as working for multiple sports teams, top-tier gyms, country clubs, fitness studios, or even private practices. I was ready to work my dream job and get paid well enough to take care of myself. I open my anatomy training book to brush up on the upper torso biomechanics.

Colin

I stared at her reply, willing it to say something else, anything else, but that.

Kittenwantstoplay: You're right, Colin...... I DON'T want to hear from you again.

Her icon was grayed out; she was offline. I can't even be upset.

I still had to surveil Jimmy for a couple more days. Tonight, I was hoping to find out what his covert operation was and then get the okay to end him. Not just for being the crime boss of Miami and a degenerate but for trying to push up on what's mi... I mean, push up on her.

Emmy

It's been days since our breakup and it still doesn't seem real. I've been having these overly sexual dreams about Colin; even my subconscious is torturing me.

Tonight's dream was so vivid. I was lying on a tropical beach, resting on my beach towel with my head on my hands as I listened to the ocean greet the land, the breeze lightly kissing my skin. The crashing sound was soothing as I rock side to side. Then I feel his hands on my upper thigh until he shakes my ass then smacks it. Leaving his mark with a bit of stinging, some pain to the pleasure. I look up and over my shoulder to see a shirtless Colin in blue swim shorts next to me. He's using those strong hands to massage the sunblock in but also copping a feel, I moan my appreciation. Being a bit obscene in a public place riles me up.

"I'm so happy you're here, kitten. I would do anything for you…"

That broke the dream, and I was mid-moan when I realized… someone was still touching me. In real life! I look to see a dark figure at the foot of my bed caressing my leg. I jumped and screamed so loud before I turned on the bedside lamp.

"AHHHHHH! WHAT THE FUCK ARE YOU DOING IN MY ROOM, YOU PERVERT! GET OUT! GET THE FUCK OUT!"

I run over to my door and flip the main light switch to indeed see Jimmy at the foot of my bed in nothing but his boxers. I immediately gag.

"No need to scream, princess. We haven't even gotten to that part yet. I was merely checking out the goods, your skin is so smooth and you smell heavenly and your moans sound so fucking insatiable. I was trying to convince you to have a bit of fun. Come on...I don't bite...unless you want me to. It sounded like you enjoyed it."

Eww. I was in my fantasy, it had nothing to do with Jimmy.

"I SAID GET OUT BEFORE I CALL THE COPS. THE FUCK IS WRONG WITH YOU?!"

By the time I finish screaming, my door opens to see all the girls looking into the room. Kayla pushed her way to the front.

"What the hell is going on? Why are you in her room, Jimmy?" She sounds calm, but her body language says otherwise.

"I woke up to him in my goddamn room, that's what!"

He holds his hands up, "Easy, easy...I got turned around. Baby, I thought that was you until she screamed."

That is complete bullshit! Kayla's room is closest to the kitchen, not set near the fence line like mine. There's no way he mixed us up.

But I watched as her face softened and she walked up and hugged him. He kisses her forehead all while staring at me. I could see she already believed his lie; she even threw a glare my way. Instead of lashing out at her ignorance, I pointed to the door, "I guess. Well, now you know where not to go. You can both leave...now!"

He smirks while brushing her hair, "Yeah, just got turned around, is all. Are you ready to go back to bed, baby doll?" Kayla smiles at his pet name for her, "Yes. Tomorrow we'll stay at your place to avoid... any confusion." She eyed me up and down before they walked out hand in hand. Most of the girls followed except Milli.

She rolls her eyes and shakes her head in disbelief, "What a load of bullshit. Your room is on the other side of the house and has a completely different layout. There's no way he could have mixed it up. He purposely came to your room like a sick pervert."

"I know Milli, but she's infatuated with him. She already believed him. I'm going to lock my door and try to get some sleep. Make sure you lock your door, too, and tell the others."

She squeezes my hand in reassurance before she returns to her room. I quickly lock my door and lean against it. What a night! I thought it was Colin touching me so intimately in my dream, but it was Jimmy.

Gross! I need a shower!

After a dip in boiling hot water and a change of clothes, I still wasn't sleepy, so I hopped on my laptop. I got a ton of comments on those photos from that night at the club, the night I broke it off with Colin.

I click my dashboard and see he's online, so I decide to video chat with him. It didn't take him long to answer, I hope he wasn't on here searching for someone new.

"Hey. Why are you up this late?"

Why is he so damn gorgeous? This is self-inflicted punishment. I could have chosen a regular chat, but I had to see him.

I can see he's shirtless again, but he wasn't in bed, perhaps sitting at a desk. A pretty small one because he was hunched over, trying to stay in the light of the tiny lamp and in front of the camera.

"I could say the same for you. It's 3 a.m. you should be getting your beauty sleep. You know, lack of sleep makes you cranky."

He's right, he's lectured me many times on the importance of sleep, but I always tried to use my big eyes to convince him to let me stay up. It never worked; what daddy says goes.

"I was asleep, until umm… never mind, it's nothing really."

Maybe I shouldn't say what happened, I started to backtrack, but he cut me off.

"That's not true, until what? It's important if you called me and brought it up. Tell me what happened, kitten. Sorry, old habits…"

I wasn't sorry he said it. I loved when he called me that. It shot a bolt of pleasure that ended between my legs and it took everything in me not to physically react or shudder.

"I was having a dream about, well, you were in it, and I thought it was you touching me in the dream but when I woke up someone was in my room touching me! I screamed bloody murder and he claims he just got turned around."

Boy, if looks could kill. He was trying to maintain his calm demeanor, but I saw right through him. His jaw was so tight it could snap. Like he wanted to snap Jimmy's neck.

"Don't lie to me, is that what you think? Who was it?"

"No, but Kayla's so damn in love or whatever she wouldn't believe a word I said. She took his side almost immediately. Jimmy has her wrapped around his finger. I just locked my door and took another shower. He creeps me out."

He shifts and I'm almost sure I heard him growl.

"I'm still in town. Do you feel safe? Do you want me to come over or you could come here?"

We have so much to work through first. I'm so unsure.

"Thanks for the offer, but I think I'm okay. I'm going to try and go back to sleep. Thank you for listening."

I saw the disappointment in his eyes. He looked away to compose himself and looked back at me with a small smile.

"No problem, I'm always here for you, Emmy. Sweet dreams."

"You, too."

Both of us hesitated to end the chat. I heard the brief pause before he called me Emmy. He didn't want to call me that, and honestly, I hated to hear it. I lay down, hoping to spend some time together in my dreams.

Colin

That prick was touching her while she slept?! What kind of sexual predator bullshit was that? I knew she liked to dress sexy for me before bed, what she had on looked modest, hopefully, the previous one was too, but I was still fuming! I hadn't even been able to touch her in that intimate way and he sneaks in and defiles her like that?

Fuck the rules. I'm going to decimate him. If I shove my gun in his mouth and pull the trigger not even dental records will ID him.

I'm glad that she turned to me when she felt afraid. Caught me by surprise, but I'm pleased. Because of everything that happened and thinking of the things I should have said, I couldn't sleep. I heard if you can't sleep it's because someone is dreaming of you. And she was, I wasn't completely off her radar, which gave me hope.

And she looked fucking insatiable, I leaned forward to deflect away from my raging hard-on and focus on what she was saying. To be that comforting ear and be there. But, when she signed off, her name slipped so easily from my lips when I came.

I am even more determined to make her mine again and this time, no lies. I will tell my little sexpot kitten, my princess, my submissive in training, that her Daddy is an assassin. I've got to put my trust in her.

Now, this assignment has become a vendetta. I needed to act fast because whatever he's into could now affect Emmy or, worse, put her in danger.

Emmy

Sure enough, the next three days following the incident, Kayla spent the night at Jimmy's. Slowly but surely, she had changed. She acts differently around me as if somehow, I wronged her when her boyfriend crept into my room. I do my best to remain civilized, no matter what, she was one of my closest friends.

Now she loves to brag about what five-star restaurant Jimmy took her to or that he chartered a helicopter and they took a quick jaunt down to Key West to see the sunset from a private white sands beach and how romantic it was.

"I have no doubt he's going to propose any day now. I know it! Oh, he's so in love with me! You should start looking for another roommate, ladies." She said as she walked out with a big smile on her face.

We all look so baffled.

What dream world was she living in?

He has never once openly said he loved her or that he even liked her, at least not in our presence. He must be feeding her the BS when they're alone because he's been consistently inappropriate with me and has had at least one incident with the others. He was living some sick, twisted orgy fantasy in his head with us.

Either way, I don't see us getting rid of him anytime soon since Kayla was so lovesick. I didn't want any animosity between us, so I'm going to stay away as much as I can. Nothing good can come from him being near me. I even bought myself a taser and had mace underneath my pillow in case he wanted to pull that lost card again. I'd empty the can and tase his balls if he touched me again.

Apparently, tonight he's taking her to dinner and after that is guy's night out. Which means she'll come back here and gloat about how much he spent on her. I definitely have to get out of the house.

Colin

I still send Emmy good morning and good night messages to let her know I'm still here and I'm not going anywhere. She sends a quick general response; I suspect to not let her current state of emotion show. Was she starting to open back up? Her responses are already more than I expected. I want to send her a text every hour of every day, but I don't want to rush it and I appreciate the interaction we continue to have as I try to build our relationship back up.

I'm still in town surveilling Jimmy's activities which have been normal to the naked eye, but it's only a matter of time. A kingpin always needs a new source of income; multiple streams of income in case one dries up or fails. Consistent money flow is their main goal.

Tonight, he took her roommate out to dinner at one of the finest Michelin-rated restaurants, Chateau Bleu and it looks like he reserved the rooftop deck for a bit of privacy. After that, they spent some time walking the pier at Fury Beach mostly looking at her phone. It looked like he was scrolling through her photos while she took in the views and clung to him. Trying to get close but he would distract her by asking a question and pointing to her phone.

After it becomes a bit too windy and chilly, he walks her back to the cars. She tries to essentially shove her tongue down his throat, but he kisses her hand before he hops in a sedan while his driver takes her home. I trail behind Jimmy until he parks at a strip club called the Spread Eagle Landing Strip.

Yeah, real classy. Nothing like a pair of giant neon, flashing legs in fishnets with a runway strip that lights from one end to in between the legs. A banner right in the middle offering 2-for-1 lap dances. If this were a barrel, we'd be scraping the bottom right about now. I bet he would never visit a place like this under normal circumstances. He was definitely here on business and not pleasure. Or at least I hope so.

With no security at the door, it was easy to follow him in. The smell of weed and cigarette smoke was suffocating and it created a hazy effect that masked the cheap interior, including hot pink bubble gum walls and black suede seating booths with gold button accents. Tacky would be an understatement for this establishment.

Jimmy walks through the main area as the dancers do their rotations, providing the patrons two minutes of pleasure for ten bucks. He slips into a hallway and I wait a few seconds in case he suspects anything. I peek around and see several doors, each with a window before the door. I use that to see if that's where he went.

I saw a few blow jobs and topless dances but no Jimmy as I neared the end of the hall. The only door left was the exit. It didn't have an alarm, if they didn't have security, I doubt they cared about the safety and well-being of others to have a fire alarm or emergency alarm door.

I cracked it enough to see it was near a dock. Jimmy is talking to some frail-looking guy in a cheap suit. "It's ten grand each Jimmy, no negotiations. No one else is providing you the quality that I am, 100% pure product."

Jimmy reaches in his jacket pocket and pulls out a stack of bills. I couldn't figure out the amount but from his partner's statement, it was at least 10k. It must be a drug deal, but we knew about his drug dealings; this wasn't his secret operation. Shit! I was so goddamn close to getting the kill order.

I requested to extend until I could put a bullet between his eyes. This bastard is mine! I was about to return to the bar and wait for him to come back and go to his next destination until…

"I know how much it is! This is the last shipment. I acquired my next batch elsewhere. Our contract is over effective immediately."

That bit of information did not sit well with his business partner, rather former partner. He took a few steps toward Jimmy, lessening the space between them. "You found another source? They can't do better for potentials than me! I find the Grade A for you. You can't do this! You can't cut me out!" The enraged man screams out, jabbing him in the chest for emphasis. Judging by Jimmy's calmness as he reaches inside his suit jacket, it was easy to figure out what his response would be.

bang bang bang

As Jimmy emptied the rounds into the man's body, I looked behind me to see if anyone would come rushing forward, but the loud music and hooting and hollering muffled the shots. Plus, I am sure they were mesmerized by the ample amounts of tits and ass on display.

"*Puta idiota!* (fucking twat) I run Miami and don't you fucking forget it! I don't need you or anyone!" He gets on his phone before walking to a shed and looking in. He reaches in and pulls out... five bound and gagged girls in white sleeping gowns. They look like they may be 18 to 22 years old, at least I hope they are of age. They were barefoot and shackled together to hinder escape.

This was it, his secret operation, trafficking girls, but to where...or whom? I hear a low hum to see a boat coming up to the dock, a profisher with two guys in all black pulling up.

"*Darse prisa!* (hurry up)"

One guy steps off the boat while the other stays at the wheel. He looks down at the man on the ground, then Jimmy.

"He's replaceable, don't worry, I already got the next lot lined up. It's amazing what people are willing to do to live the lifestyle. They cling on to any lie you tell them if you wine and dine them. Get these ones down to Havana. The next batch should be picked up soon, the girl just went back to the house to see if they were all there. We'll find another supplier later."

He takes the shackles of the first girl and pulls her towards the boat and reluctantly, they follow. I was so focused on the movement of the girls I barely noticed Jimmy walking back toward the club. I slip into one of the rooms to wait for him to pass by.

"Uhh, buddy, this room's occupied, you mind?" A guy with a girl on her knees says sternly, but she licks her lips as she stares at me like I'm next.

"Mmm, you can join us, honey. I'll even give you a discount."

She looked to be in her mid-20s, brunette with blue tips and her eyes matched her dyed ends. I swear I've seen her profile on the Sweetsugar site, her hair is very distinct. Hell, she's probably seen my profile on there. She smiles as she continues to pleasure her client with a hand job, but he definitely wanted me out.

"Sorry, man. I was trying to avoid my bookie. No can do, I have a sweet little kitten that has already claimed me as hers." Surprisingly, she chuckled, "I can tell, she's a lucky girl." I slip back out of the room. She's wrong, I'm the lucky one if she takes me back.

I looked to see that the boat was still there as they tried to position the girls down where they couldn't be seen. I snuck forward enough to tag it with a tracker and have the agency follow its journey. As much as I wanted to save them, I needed to get the exact location of where they were trafficking them to. If we get enough information, we can send in an ops team to rescue without persecution for breaking international law. The boat putters away quietly through the marsh, probably until it opens into the bay where they can punch it.

Sex trade, Jimmy was dealing in selling girls for sex. Cuba is notorious for brothels to entice both tourists and natives. How long has he been doing this? How many girls have there been? How many were underage? He profited off the disappearance of these girls and since Miami is surrounded by colleges and he owned a club, he had plenty of places to find his next...vic...tims.

FUCK!

By the time I get outside of the club, Jimmy is gone and I feel it deep in the pit of my stomach. His final words before heading back to the club replay in my mind.

"They cling on to any lie you tell them if you wine and dine them. Get these ones down to Havana. The next batch should be picked up soon, the girl just went back to the house to see if they were all there."

I drove as fast as I could to get back to my laptop. I'm closer to the hotel than her place which was 45 minutes away and time was of the essence.

I think she's in danger. I know she's in danger. I need to get to her and warn her.

Emmy

I came home and all the lights were off, weird. Usually, someone was home, or at least a perimeter light or hallway light was on. Maybe they're on a group date and Kayla is somewhere swooning over Jimmy. Blecch!

I didn't bother to turn on any of the lights in the common area. I was going straight to my room, anyway. I got a weird feeling but shrugged it off as I made it to the sanctity of my room and closed the door, turning on my music. I open my laptop and lay across my bed. Then as the website was loading, I reached back for my phone, I remember I had it on silent in the library. I lay back down and activated my screen to see 12 missed calls from Colin.

Stalker much?

I shake my head as I hear my notifications pinging like crazy. Numerous missed calls from him on the site too, what is going on? He's been very consistent since the breakup with a text in the morning and a text at night, but this was different. I rock side to side to one of my favorite songs as I ring him back. He picks up on the first ring. I'm not even sure it was a full ring he picked up so fast.

"Hey! Why so many calls? What's…"

"Kitten, where are you?! Are you in the house? Your room?"

I wanted to smile at my pet name, but he sounded, and looked so frantic. "I just got home from a long night at the library. Nobody's here, just me. Why?"

"Get out of the house. Get out of the house NOW, Emmy! It doesn't matter where you go. Just..."

The fear made me zone out as my body shuddered and goosebumps formed all over. I felt a lump in my throat, "Wh-why?" My eyes welled up with tears and I tensed up all over.

"Emmy, focus on my words. Get. Out. Of. The. Hou..."

The lights went out and my entire room was dark except for the glow of the computer and Colin looked panicked.

"Colin..." I squeaked out. I was so scared!

Then I follow as his eyes shift from me to slightly behind me on the right side.

"Someone's in your room, run!"

But before I could react, two massive arms grabbed me from behind and squeezed so hard to keep me from flailing my arms. All I could do was kick and scream and somehow hope to get them off me.

"AHHHHHH!!!! Colin! HELP! Get off me...get..." I tried to get out of their grasp when one arm disappeared, but then I felt a pinch and suddenly...the world got very dark.

"Say goodnight to your little boyfriend." Was the last thing I heard.

Help me, Colin.

Colin

I heard every torturous second of the struggle, then I think the laptop went flying to the ground because I was staring at a pitch-black screen.

A male voice told her to say goodnight and then nothing but eerie silence with the lights still out. He didn't sound like Jimmy, must be one of his lackeys doing the dirty work for him.

I quickly found Emmy's internet connection and hacked into her home security system. All the cameras were offline. I used a general code that reboots similar systems, hoping it would work. At the same time, I call the agency.

"Socrates, Zeus here, there's been an incident at a residence. 549 Pine Pinnacle, Pompano Beach, FL. I need the last two hours of footage screened up until now ASAP!"

"What happened?" I hear him typing urgently on his computer.

"I figured out Jimmy's secret operations; it's trafficking women to Cuba for their sex trade. There are probably hundreds of victims. I will send everything I know. He's been dating my girl's roommate and I think he took them because someone just attacked her in her room. I was talking to her and somebody was there in wait. I heard a struggle, then nothing. I'm trying to reboot her security cameras to see if she's still there."

I know she's not.

As soon as I said that the cameras boot up, her computer screen was cracked, and her bedding was on the floor. She probably tried to hold on to her bed and kick the perpetrator off, but she failed because she was nowhere in sight. It looks like each bedroom has a camera in addition to the common areas and perimeter.

"Socrates to Zeus, we'll scan the footage. If we find anything we will send it ASAP."

"Copy that." I toss my phone in frustration as I search the house through the camera lens. The common areas were ransacked, shattered glass everywhere, apparently, she did not realize as she went to her room. It could have saved her. I realized that as we were talking, I never heard a simultaneous struggle or screaming from the others. Perhaps they drugged the others or worse. I try not to think the worst because that could mean…

No, we are not going there. You are going to rescue them.

Then my phone rang; I crossed the room to get it.

"Zeus here."

"Zeus, we have a problem."

Emmy

*D*rip drip drip*

"Oh my god, who left the faucet on? Why do I even hear a faucet? And why do I feel so woozy?" My vision is still blurry, but I keep blinking until it finally becomes clear enough to realize...

I think I'm tied to a chair! What the hell is going on? Okay, okay let me think back, I was...talking to Colin. Yes, I remember that he had called me a bunch of times and when I finally called back, he told me to get out of the house then... someone was in my room and grabbed me!

I was kidnapped!

My head was throbbing from whatever they stuck in my neck. After a few tries, I held my head up to see Carla chained to a metal post in the corner. She stirred a bit then looked like she passed out again. Whatever they used was powerful but temporary, thank goodness.

There were no windows from what I could see and only a door. I wiggled my arms to see how much give I had, there was very little, but I noticed I was bumping into another chair. I gathered the strength to look and see Tawny and Millicent on either side of me. Thank goodness they were alive!

"Tawny! Milli! Wake up. Come on! Carla! Guys, you have to wake up!" I whisper yelled as to not alert the security guards if they were right outside the door. I rock my chair, they tied the chairs together, causing theirs to move as well. I kept calling them until I heard a groan on my left.

"Tawny! Wake up, come on, wake up! We have to get out of here. Hey, hey, hey! Come on!"

"Urgh…. what in the world is going on?! Why…why am I tied up?! Em?!"

"Calm down, breathe. I don't know what happened. I just know we're all stuck in this room. Do you see Kayla? I don't see her."

I hear Tawny's labored breathing as I feel her moving. "No, I don't see her. I see Milli. Where's Carla?"

"She's over there in the corner chained to a pole. Tell me what you remember?"

"I was in bed; I had my rain forest sound going and I was falling deeper into my sleep but then a cloth-covered hand pressed against my mouth. I panicked, inhaled, and that's it. What about you?"

I thought about it, and I felt that lump in my throat again. I wanted to cry as my heart broke. "I was talking to Colin. He was trying to warn me when someone grabbed me. I heard him say someone was in my room, but I was already struggling. Something pinched my neck and I blacked out. Oh my god, what if I never see him again?! I never got to tell him I love him. I do, Tawny. I love him."

It only took a kidnapping and the thought of dying to finally say what I was truly feeling. Why I could never pull the trigger on deleting him out of my life. That's why it was so heartbreaking to find out he was keeping secrets from me. The tears ran down my face as I shook my head. I'm going to die, and I never told him. I made such a big mistake; I wish I could take it all back.

"Hey, no, don't do that. You said it yourself, Colin saw what happened. I'm sure he called the cops and let them know what he saw. I am sure he loves you, too. Do you know how I know? Your whole demeanor changed one day, and you were the happiest you've ever been in the ten years I've known you. When you were with Dom, you were putting on a front especially when he kept hurting you but this...this was genuine. Whatever hiccup you've run into, you will work on and resolve it. When you get back into his arms, remember what's important. You and him."

Great, now I was really crying. "Thank you, Tawny. You're right. We got to stay positive; let's try to get Milli awake. Milli! Come on, wake up!" She starts moving; her head bobs, then sways side to side. She's grumbling.

"Milli, Milli! Come on, you've got to wake up!" We shake our chairs to move hers and cause her to start becoming aware.

"Wha...what? Where am I?"

"That's a damn good question that we can't answer. We just need you to wake up."

"I'm up. Ugh, I was in the kitchen when I turned around and a man in all black was behind me; he covered my mouth before I could scream, then he stuck me with something and then nothing."

"That's the same thing that happened to me, I was stuck with something, but Tawny got the rag probably laced with chloroform. We need to wake up Carla."

"Wait, where is she?"

"Don't worry, she's in my view. Carla...Carla, come on, please, you've got to wake up!"

We repeatedly call her until she's stirring. Just as she was moving around, she realized her arm was handcuffed and panicked. "What is this?! I... Why am I tied up?!" She had this look of absolute fear on her face.

"We don't know. We all woke up like this and we don't know where Kayla is or who is holding us hostage."

Just as I said that the door opens.

SON OF A BITCH!

Colin

"What is it, Socrates? I don't have time to waste."

The silence created tension that I didn't need as I replayed the moment she was taken. And there was nothing I could do to stop it. I was already scolding myself for the lies and now I had this added guilt.

No doubt in my mind I was going to leave an ocean of blood and bodies in my wake. I loaded all four of my clips with eviscerator rounds with the intent of nothing but total carnage. It was going to be a massacre.

"Zeus, Jimmy has taken the girls to his compound, but that's not the problem. His camp has identified you as one of Antonio Manelli's killers and they're looking for retribution. We don't have much time before he ships them off, we have surveillance of his compound and there's been no real movement involving the girls, but there has been an uptick of movement near the shed and dock."

My mind was racing with ways to maim Jimmy, to hear him squealing like a pig, and to butcher him like one only he would be conscious. I knew there was a chance of being identified, but how did he find out about Manelli? In fact, why does this matter?

"Wait, why is he looking for retribution for Antonio Manelli? Was he his partner or something? I didn't read about it in either manifesto."

"No, Zeus. Jimmy's government name is Matthew Manelli before he moved to Miami, he changed it to

Jimmy Gregarno to sever ties to his father's dealings and make a name for himself."

You've got to be kidding me. I killed his fucking father.

"Why wasn't I told this beforehand? Why wasn't this in any of the information you gave me?! Now that son of a bitch has my girl and her friends. She may be dead already!" My stomach drops at the thought.

"Your surveillance of Jimmy was going to be your final assignment. We were going to let one of the others finish the job. You're compromised, Zeus; your emotions have muddied your killer intuition."

I could not believe what I was hearing, but right now, I didn't give two fucks what they thought about my abilities, and I'll be damned if they take me off the case, especially not now.

I felt the darkness creeping forward, I was about to tap into a monster I had locked away long ago. I buried Daniel deep, but this entity was deeper. It crawls up from the recesses of my mind. I needed this type of darkness to become even more sadistic, cunning, and ruthless. Not caring who I hurt. I even assigned him a different code name, so the agency knew there was no going back until my beast was satisfied.

"Zeus? Say something." I hear Socrates' wavering tone.

"Zeus is no longer in control; code name Hades has been activated."

I heard him clear his throat as I put the magazines in my suit jacket and loaded the clips into the twins. I also grabbed an old friend of Hades, a set of spring-loaded ballistic knives. It was highly illegal to possess as they were basically a detachable blade that you could aim and shoot at someone. Essentially getting stabbed with the force of a shotgun blast. Hades has no sympathy whatsoever. Tonight, he was going to have free reign.

"How many people are currently on the property?"

"Umm, it looks like he has six guards securing the perimeter, and the heat scan shows about eight people inside including Gregarno. Five of them could be the girls. We'll help all we can, but once they're in international waters, you're on your own."

"They won't even set foot off the property. Hades out."

Emmy

I love you.

I should have said those three simple words long ago, but I didn't. When did I know? I'm not sure if it was when he was willing to try and learn all my curiosities or when he would send me links to dom/subpages, and he introduced me to the pet playpen. He had a vested interest in me, all of me.

Now I was staring at the man who took us.

Jimmy... and Kayla was standing proudly next to him like a goddamned trophy. She giggled and smiled while making sure half her body was touching his. Little did she know, nobody wanted Jimmy more than she did.

He shakes her off and steps forward a bit, leaving her to sway uncomfortably. "Did you guys have a nice nap? I hope so. You'll need to be alert and awake for your trip to Havana, where you'll be sold to Emillio Ruiz. He runs the brothels down there and pays top-notch for American pussy and in return I get a shipment of his brand-new cocaine/ecstasy blend. I'll flood the streets with it by morning and make a fortune because I'll be the only supplier! I'm a goddamn marketing genius!" He laughs at his great idea, but I stare daggers at both of them.

"You'll be proud to know you're each going for quite a penny, 10 grand each, except you, Emmy. I figure I'd keep you around. You're worth more here than there, anyway."

"What?! I'd rather die than be anywhere near you, you fucking psychopath!"

His grin fades into a sneer, "Don't tempt me, princess. You could have been dead the moment we stepped into your room. Could have given quite the show to your boyfriend if we murdered you while he was still on the screen. Quite an interesting tidbit of information fell into my lap. I have very specific plans for you."

Kayla's face turned to him like she was shocked by what he said. Looks like she didn't know the whole plan. She still tries to keep some sort of connection with Jimmy, it was a desperate attempt at looking significant to him.

Then our eyes locked, "Kayla, why?! Why would you do this to us, your sisters?"

She scoffs, "Huh, I am so tired of being the forgotten one! You're the smart one, the pretty one, the one people go to for advice. You made me feel like I wasn't worth any attention! Even on my birthday it somehow became all about you and your problems! It was supposed to be about me, but everybody came to your rescue when poor little Emmy came in with the big alligator tears! It probably wasn't even that big of a deal. But no matter, I purposefully sought out a man who gave me all the attention I could ever need and in return, I do whatever he wants me to. I'll be living the rich life with Jimmy while you're whoring it up with lots of men, spreading your legs for any man who has ten bucks."

Carla exploded, rattling her chain, "You did this because you weren't getting enough fucking attention?! You stupid bitch, you would sell out your friends, your sisters, so you can live the lavish life? I swear if I get free, I'll rip your fucking heart out!"

I didn't disagree with her rage-driven rant. We were all shocked and angry by her actions, but she seemed to direct her hostility toward me. She looked at me smugly while holding on to Jimmy like a trophy wife. That's probably what she wanted to be anyway, she had no real goals in life or aspirations. Her degree was a generalized one and she never seemed interested in anything more than daydreaming about the rich life.

My throat was sore from the lump that formed trying not to cry in anger, "We could have worked this out with a simple talk, not having your boy toy kidnap us and sell us into the sex trade. Do you realize how fucking insane this sounds?!"

"Correction, Jimmy is my man, not my boy toy. Emphasis on MINE, not yours! He said if he could have you guys, we would live it up, traveling the world, and we would get married! I'd never have to degrade myself to pay the bills again and my comfort is worth way more than your...friendship. Sorry, business is business."

I literally saw red as she spouted that load of bullshit, believing that a crime boss would care for her and love her. She was delusional; all Jimmy cares about is money and how to make more of it by any means.

I shake my head, too irate to respond. She laughs as she threads her fingers through his and kisses his cheek. "Right, Jimmy?"

In the blink of an eye, he pushes her, she falls off her heels onto the ground and one of his guys immediately cuffs her to the metal post by the entrance. He straightens his jacket and tosses his hands into his pockets while looking anywhere but at her.

"Jimmy... I don't understand, what are you doing?!" A nervous laugh slips her lips while trying to comprehend her current situation and save face.

He finally looks down at her and simply shrugs his shoulders, "Sorry, doll face. You're right, business IS business; when Ruiz saw your pretty little face, he offered 20K for you alone. Just think you'll be the main whore of a wealthy man. He may not even share you with his henchmen. That's about as close as being his wife."

"What?! But you...you said you loved me! That if I got them here, you'd take care of me!" Tears stream down her face.

If we were friends, I'd care about her feelings, but this is exactly the poetic justice she deserves.

He chuckles as he bends down to her level, lifting her chin up with his finger, you could see the hate and betrayal on her face when she flinched to his touch. "Carino, I never said I loved you. You were living in your own little fantasy world. I'm about my money and my business. Besides, you're...a bore in bed. You just lie there. I hear more sounds from my dog's squeaky toy when he chews it. You don't have the confidence that would make men fall on their knees at the sight of you. I can't have someone that weak next to me. I want a woman that all men want, that begs for me, and moans my name when she cums all over my dick. I need a woman who's smart, fearless, and has a mouth that spits fire and sucks me off every night before fucking me until she empties my balls. You can't suck dick to save your life."

Looks like you'll get plenty of practice soon, though. I thought to myself.

"You came every time! Explain that!"

"Yeah, well, sorry to be the bearer of bad news, but I was actually thinking about her." Suddenly his finger points at me.

What. The. Fuck.

Kayla instantly turned red in rage at his confession. I could see the jealousy all over her face.

"Her?!"

"Yes, Emmy possesses something that makes men want to approach her with purpose. She's a rare breed of woman who men want to cater to. She's exactly the type of woman I would marry."

I can't believe what I am hearing at Kayla's expense. I'm so mad at her but I'm also sad for her. He tries to touch her chin again and she jerks away in anger, "But that's not the only reason I am keeping her. She's a very vital part of tonight's plan. Now, if you will excuse me, I need to get ready. And soon you'll be on a boat headed to your new subservient lives. I'll send one of the maids in with food, she'll untie you, but my guards will be behind her with a tranquilizer gun if you feel the urge to try and run. Don't."

With that, he closes the door and leaves us in stunned silence.

Colin

Anger. Rage. Revenge. It's a bloodthirsty game of cat and mouse between Jimmy and me. His father killed my teammate, I killed his father, and I mean I personally pressed the gun to his head and watched pieces of brain matter splatter everywhere. I did resemble Hermes until I covered the evidence with my coat. The difference between Jimmy and I was I didn't broadcast it to the world.

And now, Jimmy has my girl. He's got the upper hand because he knows our relationship somehow. How he found out what I do or that I had a hand in his father's death beats me.

Did he find me on the site? Or find her and by deduction find out about us? I was on her favorites list, and she was on mine. I'm willing to bet her roommate disclosed some information and it put some of the pieces together. She probably would tell him anything to keep her status. I didn't know her but the women who cling on to the delusion of drug lords/mafia guys falling in love with them are looking to be kept.

I'm sure he'll disclose that bit of info during our confrontation.

And it's coming.

I'm outside Jimmy's compound, getting the lay of the place. He's got his own personal dock and two boats that look like they are ready for a quick departure. I should firebomb the entire compound, but I really want to put a bullet between his eyes, so I'll delay gratification.

I take a final scan of the perimeter to see if there are any unknowns they may not have caught, like guard dogs, electric fence, or even snipers. It didn't matter because Hades was going to take it all on to save the girl of his dreams. Seeing nothing he can't handle; I step out in the open towards the house.

Normally, I would sneak around to ambush each person, but Hades didn't give two fucks who saw him approach. If this were a movie, he'd walk toward the house setting off explosions behind him. Dozens of bullets flying past while he took out the bad guys with a single shot to the head or snapped their necks before he walked in and out with our girl and we'd live happily ever after, but this wasn't Hollywood.

This was a situation I never saw coming. I was in the middle of trying to make amends and I had that ripped away from me when the vendetta came back with a vengeance. This was another reason it was time to leave the agency, I put her in danger. I should have made this decision before it got out of hand, now I have to right the wrong. She was an innocent bystander, her, and her roommates. I'll never forgive myself if...

NO. We won't think that way.

I stand up, unbutton my trench coat to grab the twins from their holsters, and storm towards Jimmy's mansion. I hear movement and shouting before two guards emerge from the shack that was next to the gate. I scan to see that they are unarmed guards, a fatal mistake Jimmy made for them. Until one runs back into the shack to come out with a basic Smith & Wesson M&P9 Shield EZ. Judging by the first four shots he hadn't shot in a while if at all, I didn't even flinch. He was wildly off, but I wouldn't be. His partner panicked seeing I was still trekking towards them, screaming to shoot again but he wouldn't have the opportunity. I sent a round into one guard's chest, leaving a massive, gaping wound and I hit the other in the neck. The hole was so big he bled out before he crumpled to the ground. Two down, four outside to go according to surveillance. The cavalry rounds the corner after no doubt hearing the shots. The impact causes a small explosion, so it isn't for the stealthy kills. I wasn't looking for quiet, I was looking to set fireworks.

I made it to the gate and headed up the curved driveway when I heard shouts of, "He's at the gate!" and "Don't let him get to the house!" There wasn't as much light near the home as the road with the streetlights. I slip on my night vision glasses as it goes from dark figures moving towards me to lime green targets and I use that to my advantage as they come toward me and then stop to try to aim at me. I start to blend in with the darkness the further I move away from the streetlight, but I see them as clearly as a summer day. Hades is in the mood for a little torture and decides not to make these quick kills but to let them suffer so those inside know what they're in for. I shot a round into each man's leg and they fall beside their detached limbs writhing in pain. If they had neighbors close by their screams would cause someone to call the cops but Jimmy was typical, his house was secluded and set back away from the general traffic. There was no one around to hear their screams of anguish. I walk up slowly to each man and fire the fatal shot. Each one a different location, Hades was conducting a sick social experiment, but they all had lethal results no matter where he put the bullet.

As I head to the side of the house, I see two more bodies lying on the ground with arrows sticking out from the back of their neck and pierced through their throat.

Ares.

I couldn't see him, but I know he's high up in the tree line somewhere. I nodded in the general direction the arrows came from. I wonder how long he had been in town or if the agency sent him to finish my job because they thought I was *"compromised."*

I'm so fucking sick of that word.

I'll get the details from him later.

Now to the danger that awaits me inside.

Emmy

As Jimmy said, a petite middle-aged lady came in and untied us, placing the tray of food on the floor. It looked decent like she prepared it herself. As soon as she and the security guy left, Carla lunged for Kayla, and I put no effort into peeling her off.

Kayla screamed bloody murder as Carla wailed on her and tried to rip her hair out. "You stupid bitch, I told you I would fucking kill you! How does it feel to be double-crossed, huh? You're so damn boring no one would fuck you for free!"

Tawny and Milli are frantically trying to stop her from slamming her fist into Kayla's face over and over. Finally, I helped pull her off and to the other side of the room.

"She's not worth it, Carla! Enough!" I tried to reason, but she lunged at her again. I caught her and pressed my body against her and the wall while Tawny held her hands.

"No, she hasn't had nearly enough! Not after what she did to us! Look at where we are! You're a goddamn traitor and for what, attention?! That's the stupidest fucking excuse I ever heard. Don't sleep, bitch, or you'll take your last breath in this room, I fucking swear!" Carla slams her fist into the wall creating a hole.

To be honest, I was scared of Carla myself. I've never seen her enraged like this and it brought out a side of her I never want to be on the receiving end of. She continues to pace the room on the opposite side while Kayla holds her head up to stop her possibly broken nose from bleeding.

I ripped off a piece of my cotton undershirt. "You need to shove it up your nose to help slow the bleeding so it can coagulate." She painfully pushes the fabric up both nostrils and she lies flat on her back.

I went and split the food equally five ways and passed out the plates. I was too numb to react to any of this. None of it mattered; all I could think about was I never got the chance to give my heart to the man who made me feel special. Like I was the most important person in his world. And now there was a chance I may never see him again.

I looked at Kayla looking at us, she was pushing her food around her plate, I assumed because of the nose injury she didn't have an appetite or maybe it was guilt. She looked remorseful but there was little chance for forgiveness. If we make it out of this alive, she can pick her stuff up at the door. I guess we would need a new place, too. So many changes to be made if we make it out. So much to fix and a relationship to mend.

Colin

I decided to come in through the door that leads into the kitchen. "Hades to base; I'm headed inside." The moment I opened the door and stepped inside I knew it was wrong. It was easy. Too easy.

He knew I was here; Jimmy wasn't stupid, he obviously had the means to identify me and knew to get his vengeance, he had to take something from me. He knew I would come for her, that I would give my last breath to make sure she was safe. This could very well be a suicide mission.

Maybe she's better off.

But is she better off without Daniel? He wasn't even given a chance. Look what I put her through already, she may never want to get back together after this, and I would have to be okay with it as hard as it is to admit that.

I put my personal torment aside to observe my surroundings. There was a pot of carbonara sauce and meatballs cooling on the stove and the pasta in a Tupperware bowl. Looks like it was a family-sized portion. I heard silverware clinking and talking; they were eating dinner. I would open fire on everyone in that room. Hades will not spare one single black-hearted soul.

I attach the suppressors to the twins and have them ready for any movement.

I round the corner with guns drawn, fingers on the trigger until I see her on his lap with a gun pointed to her head. She is absolutely terrified, her tear-filled eyes silently begging me to rescue her.

Jimmy twirls the pasta around his fork nonchalantly, "You fire one shot and I'll plaster her brains all over this food, which would be a shame because Ada put so much love into it. If you're smart, you'll drop your weapons."

I didn't have a choice and I would not risk it.

thunk thunk

"Wise decision. Manny, why don't you show Mr. Wentworth to a seat."

His massive bodyguard, who was closest to me, pushed me to an empty seat at the end of the table while he continued to eat with her in his lap. She was so tense; she didn't want any contact with Jimmy whatsoever.

"Colin…" She squeaked. I wanted to tell her everything was okay but honestly, I wasn't sure. Even Colin wasn't cocky enough to believe Jimmy wouldn't pull the trigger because he would. He would have no problem shattering my world by taking her life in front of me. For this, I gladly trade my sham of a life for hers.

Jimmy extends an olive branch, sort of, by putting his gun down but his associate to the right raises his weapon, aiming at her heart, as an insurance policy. I can hear Hades growling, he's angry he can't lash out like he wants. We can't risk it.

Jimmy pauses eating to sip his wine, "Mr. Colin Wentworth, the man who came to rescue the girl of his dreams but unfortunately for him she's also the girl of *my* dreams. I've grown quite fond of little Emmy here. She's got exactly what a man like me should have in a woman, besides," He runs his fingers up her arm and she recoils, trying to get away, but he tightens his grip on her arm, keeping her planted on his lap, "we've already had some very intimate moments together, isn't that right, doll face?" He kisses her cheek and in response, she rears back and slaps him, but he's still able to hold on to her while rubbing his jaw.

He chuckles loudly, "Woo, feisty! Got to love the ones who fight back a little, right? When they finally submit, it's fucking magical. I can't wait to have this little one submitting to me and on her knees, begging to taste my release on her tongue." He shudders at his perverted thought. "Besides, aren't you a little old to have someone so young? She's more my speed, don't you think?" He brushes her hair away from her face as he raises his brow to me, "Plus, darling, having an assassin for a boyfriend is very detrimental to your health. You'll always have a target on your back. I give you exhibit A." He waves his finger between us.

She gasps as he smirks when he sees the realization on her face. He told her so easily what I'd been struggling to say for months.

I let out an audible growl and he laughed in my face. That bastard enjoyed humiliating me.

"What's wrong, pops? Did she not know? Oh..." A weaselly little sneer crossed his lips as he basked in revealing something private to her, "that's it, isn't it? Hahaha! You catfished her?! Did you post younger photos of yourself because you could be mistaken for her father! The salt and pepper hair is a dead giveaway you're well past your prime."

Now that he revealed what I was going to explain to her, I am highly irritated. And berate me like I lied about my age? I didn't, I lied about who I was, held back certain information, which is no better. I'm proud of my years that shaped me into the man I am today. I don't mind being mistaken for her daddy; I AM her daddy.

He sets his fork down and wipes his mouth with a napkin. "No matter let's get to the business at hand. After my father's brutal killing I was able to access the secret surveillance in his panic room. I took that footage and was able to positively ID you at the scene of the crime. You guys aren't as stealthy as you would like to be with all this modern technology. I think the break in the case is when her roommate introduced us at the club.

When Kayla admitted she and her friends were on a sugar daddy site I had gone onto the site to find Emmy's profile. This little kitten is quite popular on the site, but I can

why. It was strange she only had one male saved, you. Stroke of luck, huh?! I had to be sure though, so I was able to get your name from asking the right questions. Matched it against the database and here we are.

I was going to hurt you by hurting her but when I saw this little filly and how drop-dead gorgeous she was, how she radiated in sex appeal, and how every man at that club wanted to be seen with her, I decided I wanted her for myself. I kept tagging along to get closer."

It was rumored that the underworld had a database of all the assassin/mercenaries for ID'ing and Jimmy confirmed my suspicions, I can only hope they don't have any info on my real identity. Colin can go down in flames, but Daniel needed peace of mind he was safe. That should be the agency's next priority one, finding that database and destroying it. I would put that in my after-action report.

I'm startled when Jimmy slams his hands down on the table, the silverware scatters everywhere and causes Emmy to jump. "Did you know he was my father when you tortured and killed him like an animal?"

I didn't even hesitate to respond, "I enjoyed every delicious minute of it. Who knew there was so much blood within the human body? I mean you know how much is in there from science but to see it all pooled up on the outside of a human body. It's quite brutal." I leaned forward to catch him trying not to break character but to know I gutted his father like a pig caused his eye to twitch. "His screams were the icing on the cake, you know?" I just smile, "He was a low-life piece of shit, and the trait must be hereditary. My teammate knew you could be a threat, but I ignored it. I should have come down here and wiped you off the face of the Earth. But no worries, I'm going to make it a family tradition when I watch you take your last struggling breath like your daddy. It's amazing how even the most hardened criminal shows absolute fear in their eyes before they die."

Then he does the unthinkable, he snatches her by her hair, pulling it hard enough for her to scream out in pain and it sends chills down my spine. He reaches in his coat pocket and pulls a straight razor, pressing it against her throat. I could see she was trying to stop breathing or calm it so it wouldn't aid in cutting her open.

"You think you're funny, it won't be so funny if the last thing you saw was your precious Emmy being sliced open. I'll make sure to defile her before I slit her ear to ear!"

Hades was chomping at the bit, but we needed to act methodically not emotionally. "Is that the only way you get to touch something so special, by violating her? I'll tell you this, you will never put your hands on her inappropriately again, Jimmy. Sneaking into her room, watching her while she slept, and touching what's mine. You might think I'm too old to keep up with someone so young, but she can tell you...I am more than capable. That stunning beauty has changed my entire outlook, has made me see that settling down is the right thing to do because I want to spend my life with her. It doesn't matter about our age difference or what we like to do when we are alone. It's just her and me, no one else matters. And if by a stroke of the worst luck I happen to lose my life tonight, I want her to know that I love her. Not as Colin, but as Daniel. Daniel loves Ember and if I make it out alive, I will do everything in my power to make it up to her."

It didn't matter if Jimmy knew my real name, he wouldn't live past tonight to relay that bit of information. None of them would, not even the maid. There was a silence; I never took my eyes off her as I watched the tears fall when she took in every syllable I spoke. Then her lip started to quiver.

Emmy

He poured his heart to me and everyone at the table. I was shocked and all I could repeat in my head at that moment was his name, his actual name.

Daniel

Now that I look at him, he does look more like a Daniel and not Colin. There was something missing about Colin and my guess is that Colin was sort of the protector to the real him. His intense gaze as he spoke every syllable with the passion of a man madly in love set my body on fire, how I wanted him to show me how much he loved me.

But let's go back to what Jimmy said, he's an... assassin?! Like, he kills people for a living?! Now that I had a chance to think about it, it starts to make sense. The constant travel, getting rid of his phone, always wearing suits, making sure not to create a trail back to him, and being able to provide enough funds to support me. He may have been lying but now I know why, and my reaction seems so childish in perspective. He really did lie to protect me, plain and simple. Why? Because he killed bad guys for a living. The man who has my heart was an assassin.

I'm brought out of my thoughts when he sat up and leaned forward to place his arms on the table. Jimmy's henchman's gun follows his movement. He literally could blow him away in front of me, but he wanted to make sure I knew he loved me.

"I love you…" I choked out because I was so upset at the current situation. What should have been spoken in an intimate moment between us was forced to light by the danger of our situation. We were both at the risk of losing our lives.

"Isn't that touching, boy meets girl and falls in love, but that's not going to keep me from killing you and taking her to avenge my father's death. I have plans to broadcast your death just like my dad did with your colleague. Then my enemies will know not to fuck with the King of Miami! No one will have the balls to cross me!" He laughed, making me move along his lap closer to his groin. Immediately, I scoot to the edge to avoid any type of intimate touch. I was disgusted to be a pawn in his mind games against Colin, I mean Daniel.

"How well did that go for your daddy, Jimmy? Not too well before I put a bullet between his eyes! How hard was it to identify what was left of him? Hmm?" He arched his brow, and I could feel Jimmy growling internally.

Suddenly he shifts his leg, causing me to lose my balance and tumble to the ground. "Get her ready with the others. Just for that, I'll make sure she has front row to your demise." He looks down at me." It would be in the best interest of your friends that you convince them to go quietly. I won't hesitate to execute them in front of you. Take her now!"

The guard grabs me by my arm aggressively, shoving me toward the entrance into the living room and the hall where we were being kept. I try to turn around to lock eyes with my beloved.

"Colin…"

"It's okay, kitten." He nodded and for some reason, it calmed me.

I hope he had a backup plan. I know he didn't mean to get caught...or did he?

Colin/Daniel

Hades wanted to unleash hell, but we couldn't do that with a .357 magnum aimed at our vital organs. I would play the part of being "caught," but they failed to search me or pat me down, an amateur mistake; they only took the weapons they saw me drop. I still had the ballistic knives on my person.

"So, Jimmy, or would you prefer Matthew? Listen, I don't have the patience for the back and forth so, let them go. You don't want them; you want me and here I am. We're going to settle this, and it will end with me stomping on your windpipe until you meet your father in Hell." I lean back and raise my brow in confidence. I couldn't wait to unleash Hades.

He laughs again, this time a bit more sinister than the last. "Sorry, Ruiz is expecting his shipment and I need that new drug flooding the market by morning. They'll be hooked by nightfall, and I'll be swimming in cash in a couple of days and you... you'll be a pile of ashes on the ground." He snaps his fingers and two of his men surround me. "Now, put him in the same room as the girls so he can say goodbye. You're going to die a slow, painful death. It will be you meeting my father in Hell."

Before I could reply I felt a sharp pain in my temple as the world went black.

Emmy

The guy pushes me harshly back into the room. The girls rush to help me up.

"Emmy, are you okay? What happened, what did he do to you?!" Milli looked me over and I shook my head. "I'm fine." I notion for her to follow me to the corner on the opposite side away from Kayla. Carla and Tawny followed; it was an unspoken understanding.

Kayla was facing away and hadn't tried to make a move towards us. She was probably still scared of Carla killing her with her bare hands. She knew she was on her own and that we were no longer her friends.

I couldn't stop the smile from forming if I tried.

"Colin's here! He came to rescue us, isn't that great?!" I giggle as the words spill out.

"Is he insane?! He's going to get killed, Emmy! What can he do against Jimmy's security and whatever measures he has in place? You said he was a freaking salesman. What can a salesman do?"

"I lied. Well, he lied to me, but he's not a salesman." I see Kayla perk up when she notices that we are huddled together and talking in hushed tones. I pulled Tawny and Carla closer so she couldn't see or hear my next words.

"He's going to save us; I can't go into detail, but you have to trust me." They could only trust the words I spoke. I put my finger to my lips to tell them to keep quiet.

Kayla wasn't our friend and any information she could muster she would probably run to Jimmy to get back in his good graces. We all know where her loyalty lies. It's sad and pathetic.

The rest of us sit in the corner and huddle together for warmth. I had to put faith in the man who told me he loved me. He would come at any moment to take us away from this nightmare.

Then the door opens, and I see Colin limp and being dragged into the room. They toss him on the floor and a puff of dust formed after he exhaled from the force of being dropped.

"Colin!" They slam the door and I try to turn him over. "Someone, help me! Colin, baby, wake up. Co-..." He wasn't responding, then I saw the bruise on his temple; they must have hit him there to knock him out. I brush my fingers across his face, but he doesn't stir. I'm panicking.

"Daddy, please... wake up. I can't do this without you." I whisper cry and lean forward to cradle him against me. I finally had him in my arms, but not like this, not like this.

I kiss his forehead and brush his hair back in place, "Please. I love you. The other stuff doesn't matter, just... wake up." I kissed his lips, finally feeling him on mine, but there was no reciprocation, and it broke my heart. I choked on a sob as I watched a tear fall from my eye and hit his cheek. Everyone watched me while I felt lost and defeated.

"Well, it's about time I felt those beautiful lips on mine." His eyes open and he winces before he smiles. "Hi, kitten."

I didn't mean to blurt it out, it was a lot in such a short moment. "I'm sorry, I'm sorry I left, that I didn't let you explain, that I was so stubborn and childish. I don't want you to leave. I want to be in your arms. I'll follow you wherever; I don't care; just don't leave me!"

He holds his head while sitting up, then he notices our audience. "Well, I suppose this is your version of meeting the parents. Meet the roommates. Hello, ladies."

"Hi!" They exclaim while grinning from ear to ear.

I introduce them as he wipes my tears away. "This is Carla, Tawny, and Millicent."

He nods, "Nice to meet you. Emmy, look I…"

"No! Don't call me that. I hate it when you call me that!" I wrap my arms around him and squeeze tightly, but I felt a strong open-handed swat as a warning for telling him no and for yelling. Or at least that was my guess.

"Under these circumstances, I'm going to ignore that little outburst. I know you don't like it, but if I need to have a serious conversation with you, I promise, then and only then will I call you Ember or Emmy. What I was trying to tell you in the hotel room was that I'm going to retire. The agency labeled me compromised and they are right; I am. I fell in love with you and I don't regret it. It's time I finally settled down and lived my life as Daniel Allen Denning."

OMG.

I burst out laughing, almost hysterically and everyone was looking at me, even Kayla. I wave my hand, "I'm sorry, it's just that your initials are DAD!" He chuckles as he pulls me in and our foreheads touch before he glances over my shoulder.

"What about her?"

I didn't have to even move to know who he was talking about. The question triggers Carla, "Oh, you mean that dumb, traitorous bitch in the corner? It's because of her that we're in this mess, isn't that right?! She sold us out to get attention from a man who sold her stale ass to the highest bidder!"

Yeah, she's still violently angry. It's like he stepped on an emotional landmine. I try to neutralize the situation.

"Kayla set us up under the guise that Jimmy would take care of her and live the lavish life. But never mind her."

Then we heard the locks on the door being unlocked.

"Don't say anything, kitten." He goes limp in my lap. I had to force myself not to smile hearing his nickname for me. The doors open and two men come in, one holding a stack of cloth.

"Put these on before we take you to the boat."

The other one nudges the guy who spoke, "Huh, he's still knocked out, shame. He'll be quite surprised when he's the only one left in the room. Get dressed!" His voice boomed in the tiny room. He crosses his arms in a silent tone of dominance.

Eventually, they realized we wouldn't get dressed while they were looking, so they left and locked the door.

Tawny picks one up. It's a thick white sleeping gown, long sleeves with ruffles and high necklines, the kind you see in cults. It made it look like the women were pure and virginal, but I'm sure they didn't care down there. It was some sort of sick fantasy.

"Put them on. I have a plan." He interrupts my disturbing thoughts. I didn't expect him to say that.

"What?! No, Colin, that's crazy! You want us to go with them?"

"Daniel," He corrects me then steps closer, "it's daddy to you, little one, and don't you forget it. I believe one of my teammates is here. There's a possibility the others are here, too. I have to appear weak and vulnerable to make this work, they'll lower their guard. Trust me."

His eyes beg me to comply, and I growl. Once again, he taps my ass for talking back. This is going to take some practice; I hope he has enough patience for me as I learn. I looked at him shocked, but I reluctantly agreed.

He puts himself in a corner so the other girls can change out of his view, but I slide in front of him and strip down, my eyes never leaving his until he can't take the pressure and looks down. Of course, I had on something racy, a black lace set with thigh garters. I loved wearing the sexiest lingerie under my regular clothes. I watched him leering at me, but it wasn't disgusting like when Jimmy did it. It was full of promise. I saw the slightest uptick in the corners of his mouth.

"You like, Daddy?" I wink and he groans painfully. "Under different circumstances, absolutely, but that garter may work to our advantage. Put the gown on."

As I pull the fabric over and it clears my view, I realize he's unbelievably close and I can't move because I'm now against the wall and I squeak. He looks around to see everyone was purposefully avoiding looking our way. I felt vulnerable underneath his gaze. He reaches under his pant leg to reveal two...oddly shaped knives?

"They are ballistic knives; think of a gun with a knife as a bullet. You aim and press this button, be careful, it has a hair-trigger, and you only get one chance.

He slides the knife tip lightly over the gown between my breasts and over my right hip as he lifts the gown up to slide the blade gently into the garter. I took the other one and slipped it on the other side. I couldn't take another teasing; I'd burst into flames or shamefully orgasm to his slightest touch.

I quickly clear my throat and drop the gown. "What are you going to do?"

"Play possum, baby." He gives me a reassuring smile, but I need to address the elephant in the room as I look over to the other side of the room.

There's so much animosity between us and Kayla, but we'll need her to cooperate and not turn on us and botch the plan. I need to extend the olive branch.

As much as I want to scream fuck her because of the magnitude of trouble she put us in, I know we can't have any outliers. I tilt my head in her direction. "I need to get Kayla to go along with the plan. We don't need any surprises that could work against us. I guess I can hate her later." I groan internally at how much I didn't want to.

He places his hand on my face and I bask in his touch, his strong yet gentle touch.

"Yes, you can hate her later but right now I need you to be a good girl. Can you do that for me?" He didn't have to say anymore, I wanted to make him proud of me.

She had her legs pulled up and her arms around them with her head down. I felt the tiniest bit of sympathy.

"Kayla?"

She looked at me, her eye was turning black where Carla punched her and her nose was now swollen, but the bleeding had stopped. She had used water and her old clothes to clean her face of blood. I sat next to her and she jerked in reaction.

"You're not going to hit me, are you?"

"No, I am going to put those feelings aside because no matter how I feel about what you did to us, we need you to help us all escape. We can deal with the aftermath later. I need your cooperation and solemn vow that you won't turn on us again."

She rubs her jaw, "I realize my mistake, I got it beat into me. I was stupid and foolish to think that someone like him would love me. I did all that and for what? I lost you guys, the closest thing I had to family. He doesn't want me; now nobody does. Everyone wants someone like you. You have a man over there who adores you and is willing to risk his life for you. I want that. I want to find someone who genuinely cares for me."

I put my arm around her and hugged her tight. "Don't compare yourself to me. You have plenty of good qualities that a man will find amazing. You will find someone after you seek help for your issues, but we can work on that later. Are you with us?"

She looks at the girls standing behind us. I can still see she's afraid of Carla and Carla is still upset, but for this plan to work we all need to work together.

Tears flood her eyes, "I'm sorry! I know it doesn't mean much, but I am! I'll help any way I can." I squeeze her hand for reassurance as I turn to Daniel.

"Okay, we're ready."

Colin/Daniel

After going over the plan and just-in-case scenarios, I place one final kiss on her lips, "We'll finish what we started later, kitten." She blushed as I squeezed her ass under that white gown. It had all the disturbing traits of a cult recruiting innocent girls. The floor-grazing fabric, the high necklines, ruffled sleeves, and that white baptismal tone. I don't know what sick angle they were playing, but I was going to shut down this entire operation and hopefully rescue the victims already down there.

She purrs under my gaze, "Yes, daddy." She hugs me and holds me tight; she's scared and worried because there are so many moving parts. I think I have an idea about Jimmy, but only time would tell. I break the hug and give her a comforting smile before laying back on the floor. She kneels beside me while holding my hand.

Just as we got settled, the door slammed open, so much they all screamed. I peek to see them barge in wearing all black with semi-automatic weapons in their hands, to intimidate them to comply.

"Let's go! Everyone out!"

"You can't leave him like this! He hasn't moved since you threw him in here, you monsters! He could be really hurt."

Give my princess an Oscar for her award-winning performance chock full of angst, emotion, and desperation. I try not to react but I'm so proud of her.

I felt the movement of her being moved from beside me. I couldn't tell if it was forcefully but judging by the stream of curse words coming from her, it was.

"Good, maybe his death will be effortless if he can't fight back. And when boss gets tired of you and tosses you to the side for a fresh piece of ass, I get first dibs."

Then I hear the door slam behind them. I'm still unsure if Ares is the only member here. It's very rare we all get called to the same job, but this was becoming an agency priority. No one in this compound was going to relay anything and it would die on Jimmy's last struggling breath.

Emmy

Jimmy was waiting outside of the patio doors by the path that led down toward the docks. He separated me from the group as they walked ahead with his goons and now, I was at his side. We stopped by the warehouse next to the docks.

Inside the rundown building were all the indicators of a drug lab, propane tanks near each station, different tools used to cook and package the product like test tubes, burners, and safety equipment. There was even some loose product lying around. The smell was so powerful it made my eyes water and I started gagging.

"How does it feel to be in the arms of the richest man in Miami? Look around, this could all be yours and you would want for nothing."

"Is that what you think this is about, money and power? I'm not Kayla. I don't care about a man's bank balance. It's about his heart and yours doesn't exist."

"Then why were you on a sugar daddy site? All you women care about is money, someone to spoil your ass rotten while you sit back and do nothing. Hell, you don't even cook or clean."

"I'm not going to sit here and argue with you. You've already made your mind up about women like me. We're just money-grabbing, attention-seeking whores, so why don't you let me get on the boat with my friends because I'd rather suffer the days sleeping with random men for pesos than the thought of you touching me in any way!"

Jimmy laughs as if I made a joke, "No chance, sweetheart. Although I could probably get at least $50K for you, I'd rather have you under me at night because eventually, you will fall to your knees before me and worship me like the god I am! But first, you're going to watch your old man burn alive while we broadcast it to the dark web."

He points to a small open area I hadn't noticed before. I see a post in the middle of a pit surrounded by stones and filled with sticks and hay. Not too far away was a clearly marked gas canister next to a video camera on a tripod. He WAS going to broadcast setting him on fire! I wanted to scream and fight back to avoid any part of this happening, but I had to remember the very strict orders he gave me. No matter what I saw, I had to keep calm and wait for my cue.

I didn't even acknowledge Jimmy's last statement looking away and keeping my eyes on my friends. They looked terrified as the two men flanked them.

Jimmy takes a radio out, "Bring our star to the stage." He places the radio back in his jacket pocket, laughing at his own sick joke.

I watched as they drug a limp Colin down the hill and they stopped in front of me. He still wasn't responding, "Colin…" I could only squeak out his name before I felt that cold lump in my throat.

"Tie him up." They drag him over to the post, tie his hands behind the pole, and anchor his waist with the rest of the rope, his top half hung forward slightly. His usually coiffed hair hung forward messily and he still wasn't moving. I was beginning to doubt if he was acting and thought maybe they roughed him up when we were out of sight. He really could be hurt!

By the time I could focus back on reality, I noticed that we were up there by ourselves, and the girls were closer to the boat.

"So darling, you have a choice, either watch him die or watch the boat leave with your friends. Both will happen at the same time so choose wisely." His hand slides from my back down to the top of my ass where he rests his hand. I want to break his fucking arm off; I want to kill him with my bare hands, but I step away, so his hand drops but he immediately grabs me by my hair and I scream.

"Let go of me!"

"I'm not going to keep fighting with you! How about I kill them all and slit your fucking throat?"

"It's better than having you near me, *maldito monstruo* (you fucking monster)." Before I could react, the hand wrapped around my hair pushed me into his lips as he kissed me aggressively. Then he pushed me off and I tumbled to the ground, trying my damndest not to puke my guts out. He tasted like an old cheap cigar.

"You're one feisty kitten, even your angry Spanish is sexy, but you didn't answer me..." He reaches in his jacket and I am now staring down the barrel of his gun. "Which one?! You have 30 seconds to think about it or...I may execute you in front of him. The pain he would feel if he saw your precious little head blown off.

I had to think quickly. I had to stick as close to the plan as possible to make sure it worked. I conjure up some tears and look up at Jimmy pathetically, "I want to say goodbye to him. I can't leave him like this, please." I wipe my tears away and sniffle.

He lowers the gun, "Wow, that's the type of loyalty all men in power look for. I expect the same. Now get up!" I am pulled up by my arm to my feet by his lackey. The other surrounded Colin's feet with wood and brush, essentially building the bonfire around him.

My anxiety was at heart attack level because I had yet to see him move, I couldn't even see the rise and fall of his chest to know if he was even breathing.

What if he was already dead?! What if they killed him when he was all alone? My heart couldn't take all these negative thoughts. I wish this whole situation could have been avoided. Could this all have been avoided? Who knows, but now I may have to literally watch the love of my life die right in front of me.

And then, he gasped! He held his head up for a moment before letting it drop back down.

"Colin!" He didn't respond. The goon rips his shirt open and I can see his chest heaving like he had been held underwater. He was alive!

I look back to see the girls sitting on the boat's floor as they remove the rope from the dock getting ready to depart. I wish I could be at two places at once, but my attention is brought back to Colin as he groans when the guy throws something on him, and even from as far away as I am, I know what it is, the scent is undeniable.

Gas.

My head is spinning! I'm witnessing a nightmare and I can't breathe. They are going to set him on fire and broadcast it live. The goon stands behind the camera as

Jimmy pulls me close to the bonfire site; the scent is almost unbearable. It must burn and could cause irreversible damage to his beautiful skin. The skin I never got to run my hands down before I slipped my delicate fingers into his pants and watched his eyes roll back in response to my touch. The skin I wanted pressed against me, feeling the heat radiating from his body to mine. It all made me think about what could have happened had I not blown up at him and walked out. I'll never forgive myself for this.

I look back and the boat is out of view and my heart sinks. I couldn't save them and now they were in more danger than before.

"Hey, eyes front and watch the show, I won't tell you again!" Jimmy holds his arms out and points at his henchman, "Hey! Are we live? Good." He does a dramatic entrance into the camera view. "Welcome dark web exclusive members to a live execution. This is in honor of my father, the great Antonio Manelli, who those bastards massacred. I always say an eye for an eye, so here we are about to roast one of the men who killed my father. Why do you ask?! So that all my enemies know not to fuck with Jimmy Gregarno!" He sounds like a pompous douchebag and he makes me physically sick. I'd rather die than live my life with him. His grin is a mile wide as he waves his gun in Colin's direction. "That's right, my competition should know that I have no problem torturing you in front of the masses then take over your territory! Now, before we burn him alive, let's make sure he's alert and cognizant to get maximum reaction.

Colin/Daniel

I've been cognizant the whole fucking time listening to this piece of shit, Hades is in complete control now and the bloodbath is about to begin.

Cocky and arrogant but not too bright Jimmy and his crew already made several fatal mistakes. The first was tying my hands behind my back and out of their view, it is easier to manipulate the hands and loosen the rope. They hitch-tied me to the post but did not raise me a few inches off the ground to hinder mobility. From what I can feel as I rub my wrists together and get my fingers around the rope, they used a simple handcuff knot, imagine the rope version of handcuffs and like handcuffs, can be easily manipulated.

As he bragged and gloated about his barbaric family tradition, I had loosened the rope enough to look like I was tied, but I was holding the slack. Another mistake was that they looped the binding at my waist to the cuffs so that it was also loose and ready to burst out of.

I was letting him enjoy the fanfare. It's like it is in the movies, revealing your entire plan before you execute it. It never ends well.

My head teeters left and right to look like I was still out of it and then I lift my head and open my eyes. A quick scan and I had a layout of the immediate area. As soon as I looked back up, his lackey landed a hard right to my jaw and my head shifted left. I spit out blood as I hear Emmy scream for me.

No worries, kitten. I've taken worse punches. This guy was all bark and no bite. He stood a good six foot six, a few inches taller than me but his swing was weak; all he did was further piss Hades off. So essentially, I was free just waiting on the right time and then Jimmy did something so fucking stupid. He placed my guns on a table by the shed, only a few feet away from where I was. He turns to me, "Wonder what type of ammo you assassins used because I couldn't even identify my father except by dental records and DNA!"

Like father, like son, Jimmy, keep talking.

Hades growled as Jimmy pulled the magazine to inspect the rounds. The eviscerators looked like normal rounds until fired, there was a chance he could shoot me with one, but I kept my cool for her sanity. I know her eyes have never left me.

Then he points my gun at me, right between my eyes. "I should blow your brains out and end it quickly, but I want you to suffer, suffer as my dad did! Besides, my audience is paying good money to see a torturing. Oh yes, there's always a way to make money. Maybe…" I watch his aim lower and is now locked on my dick. "Not like you'll get to use it anyway, but maybe I should let her watch you become a eunuch in your final moments."

I held my breath. I was like any other man; it is precious cargo and losing it is detrimental to life. Even Hades was hesitant to move until Jimmy placed the gun on the table. He picked up the same gas canister his goon had earlier and began pouring it near my feet.

"You're going to burn and I'm going to make sure she watches every single second." He empties the can but saves some to splash in my face and luckily, I closed my eyes in time to avoid the burn. I shake my head furiously to get most of it out of my face but that doesn't dull the acrid smell.

"Any last words, you pathetic piece of shit?!" He stares into the camera before a lit torch comes into view and is handed to him.

I chuckle, "Yeah, Jimmy, one thing…"

A few minutes later, there's a lot of blood, a fire, and I am lying on the ground.

Emmy

"...Now, Emmy!" It all happened so fast I felt like I was watching it as a movie. As soon as he said that all the ropes fell from his body. Jimmy was confused, seeing that he was so quickly free that he didn't even notice me aim the ballistic knife. He didn't react until the blade was wedged in the middle-left quadrant of his back. It shot with so much force the kickback was similar to the Glock I shot at the range last year. I am glad it hit the target.

"UGH!" He turned around as he grunted, his eyes were wild as I dropped my dress back down from pulling it up to retrieve the knife.

"You stupid fucking whore! I'm going to kill you!"

Even with the knife lunged in his back, he was able to rush me and wrap his hands around my neck. I stomped his foot and kicked him in his testicles, but he kept the tight grip around my neck, and I was starting to panic. I couldn't even call out for him. Then I was on the ground struggling.

"*Puta de mierda!* (fucking whore), you're going to pay!" He holds both my hands in one hand. I see him reach into his jacket and then I see a flash, hear a gunshot, and feel a growing searing pain. I realized, milliseconds after he straddled me so I couldn't move, that he shot me. My arm was on fire as I saw the sleeve and side of the ground turning red from the bleeding. I was lightheaded from that and shock. Then I heard Jimmy cock his gun for a fresh round in the chamber. He aimed it at me, his target ranged from my head to my shoulder and neck from him swaying so much. I assume from his own blood loss.

Where was Colin?! I felt myself fading in and out, I'm too weak to fight him but I won't make it easy. Jimmy smiled and it was coated in blood, confirming that I had pierced his lung; he was going to drown in his own blood but not before he killed me.

I close my eyes and await my tragic fate

Remember that I love you...Daniel.

bang

The sound was so loud my eyes shot open. I heard Jimmy grunt before he fell forward against me like a tree cut down in the forest. I wiggle, but he doesn't move; he's out cold...or dead. I look up to see someone holding something in their hand. My vision is blurry and I'm so tired.

"Emmy! OMG, get off her, you bastard!" I blinked a few times, the voice sounded like... my vision clears to see Kayla with a metal pipe in her hand that she threw down to help me.

The huge weight is rolled off my body enough to breathe again but it hurts so bad like I'm inhaling molten lava. I look over to see I lost a lot of blood. I lay my head back to the center.

"Emmy, hold on!" She places her hand to cover my wound and presses hard. I scream out my pain. There was so much movement around me, but I couldn't focus. And I couldn't breathe without coughing, I think something was on fire because there was smoke everywhere. I could only hope that my Daniel was okay.

Daniel, I love you.

Assassinated by Love

And then it was dark and the pain was gone...

Colin/Daniel

Once I dropped the rope and gave Emmy the cue, she shot the blade into his back, hopefully piercing something vital. It was way better than I had hoped for because the pressure released was like a regular round and could have thrown her trajectory way off course. I needed him distracted while I disposed of his henchman. Jimmy drops the torch near the shed in a pile of grass and it starts a fire. I, on the other hand, am trying to get to my weapons. His henchman reaches me before I could get to the table and slams me on the ground.

bang

I didn't have enough time to figure out what that was as he was trying to cave my face in. Hades is over it. I reach down while trying to block and push him off me to reach for the knife.

clang

Another sound I'd have to figure out later as I am able to reach the knife and fire it into his chest. He grunts and looks down as he grips the handle that was deeply embedded into his breastplate, it was in a good four inches. No way he was getting that out, but he was trying. I push him over and scramble to my guns and fire two rounds, one into his chest leaving a gaping hole large enough for the knife to fall out and the other struck his arm, tearing it to shreds. I only needed one shot, but Hades wanted the bloodbath he was owed, one down, one to go. Gurgling was the last sound from him before his gaze went icy cold. I look around to assess the situation and I see that Kayla girl crouched down pressing against something and I see another pair of legs...Emmy!

Before turning around, I heard two shots ring out, which confirms it was a gunshot I heard earlier. I look back and see Jimmy raised up with smoke billowing from the gun and Kayla was now face down on Emmy's body. Then there's no movement from either of them.

I felt as if Hades had separated from me and was next to me trying to relay what I already knew.

Whispering in my ear:

She's dead.

She's gone and it's all Jimmy's fault. He killed your princess, your kitten, the love of your life. Make him squeal!

Internally I was screaming, mourning the loss of the girl who saw through it all and still loved me, and now...

In a blind rage, I shot Jimmy in the leg causing pieces of it to explode into the air, coating me in a thin layer of retribution. His foot was barely hanging on by the ligaments. I pressed my foot down on the leg remnants and smiled fiendishly. My sanity was long gone now.

His ear-piercing screams and suffering were satisfying to Hades, but it also distracted me, and I didn't realize it until I felt two burning sensations and my body jerked involuntarily. I look down and see Jimmy aiming his gun at me until he couldn't hold himself up any longer.

I choked and spat out blood. I look down and see blood coming from my upper leg and from below my shoulder.

Jimmy's struggling to breathe, judging by the blood seeping in the front, his lungs are filling with blood, but he still has that smug smile as he laughs as if he was dragging me down with him. I stand over him, feeling woozy from my own injuries but I try not to show weakness.

He wheezes while coughing, "I took her from you and that's better than you dying! You took someone from me and I... I did the same. Maybe I'll get her on the other side and she'll be mine for eternity!" He chokes as he struggles to laugh.

Rage washed over me as a flash of heat overwhelmed me. I didn't even have the words to tell him I hope he rots in Hell next to his father. I guess those were the words, but instead, I unload half the clip into his body. I couldn't even tell where the bullets penetrated his body because what was left was something so gruesome it shocked Hades into silence. He retreated into the depths of my mind.

I don't know if the adrenaline was catching up or if it was the grisly scene of the remnants of Jimmy, but the world spun out of control and suddenly, it went black.

Please, I just want to be on the same plane of existence to see my princess again. Life or death...it doesn't matter, I need her...

Emmy

*B**eep...beep...beep*

That's annoying! What is that?! Why is it so loud?!

It takes all my energy to open my eyes and immediately I flinch to the stark white lighting. It's so bright for no reason! I groan and am startled by sudden movement on my right.

"It's Emmy! She's awake. Go get the doctor, an orderly, somebody! Emmy, it's Carla! Can you hear me?!"

I shield my eyes, "No need to shout. I'm not deaf, woman. Where am I?" I pushed myself up with my good arm as much as I possibly could. I didn't need her to answer; it was obvious I was in the hospital.

A doctor comes in, "Ah, Miss Peters, so glad to see you awake and alert. Tell me, from 1 to 10, what is your current pain level?" He asks as he takes down my vitals.

"Sitting at a solid 9 and three-fourths, doc." What did he expect me to say? I feel spectacular, just peachy! I'm a bit snippy so I keep the rest of my snide remarks to myself.

"Alright, I'll get the nurse to give you something to take before your dinner."

I look around for a clock or maybe see the date or time scrolling on the tv. "What time is it? What day is it? I don't remember what happened after..." I stopped because the memories were pouring in, I needed to know what happened after I blacked out.

He flashes a light in my pupils, further blinding me and causing my eyes to water. He quickly jots something down. "You came in with a gunshot wound to the shoulder. We took you into emergency surgery to remove the bullet and stop the severe bleeding." He looks at his watch, "It is currently 8:42 pm on Wednesday."

"Wednesday?! I've been unconscious for four almost five days?"

I notice Carla, Tawny, and Millicent next to my bed now. They all were wiping away tears.

"We thought we lost you!" Carla couldn't stop bawling at the thought of my almost dying. I reach for her and squeeze her hand.

"Hey, I'm okay, don't cry, I'm going to heal at home and you can take care of me." I break the tension by making them laugh and they surround me, cocooning me in their warm embrace.

"It'll be some time before you can go home, I want to make sure you are healing properly and there are no complications. I'll get started mapping out your prescriptions and instructions to have when you are released. Get some rest, Miss Peters, you've been through quite an ordeal."

I could only nod as a sharp pain shot through my arm and I hissed through my gritted teeth. I hope they prescribe the good stuff to tolerate pain like this. What a night that was...wait!

"Where's Colin? I mean Daniel?" I shake my head as they look at me with raised brows. "It's a long story, but where is he? You know who I mean!"

They look at each other and I see Tawny fidget with her hands, a sign of nervousness. You learn a lot about people's behaviors when you live with them. I also took a few courses so that when I have clients, I could tell when they were anxious or nervous while I worked on their bodies.

A feeling of panic washed over me, "What are you not telling me?" They continued their awkward silence while they communicated non-verbally to each other. I felt my stomach drop, and the tears instantly formed. I just assumed...

"No.... please..."

I shook my head and closed my eyes to shut off the world, I desperately wished I could turn back time. This is a living nightmare, my life would never be the same and all I wanted was to be with him, to spend our lives together after his retirement. I even had a passing thought of a family together, him running around the yard after our son...and now...all I have are dreams.

"Oh no, Emmy, he's not dead! We don't think. It's that we don't know where he is. We asked and described him, but we only had his first name, names, and they said he was in a restricted part of the hospital and no information was to be given. We really did try to find out for you before you woke up."

I laughed nervously while patting Tawny's hand. I am so happy they tried. I exhaled so loudly, but the tears still ran down my cheeks because I still had no clue about his status.

"You almost gave me a heart attack! How am I supposed to know if he's okay? I can't sit here. He needs me!" I felt the hopelessness consume me. I didn't even hear my door open, but I heard someone clear their throat.

"Perhaps, I can be of assistance." A rather tall redhead in a three-piece suit stood there after it closed behind him. After recalling all of Colin's behaviors, I am almost sure, he too, is an assassin.

I notice I am the only one tensing up as he approaches. The girls seem to be okay in his presence.

"Ladies, good to see you again. Allow me to introduce myself; my name is Hermes."

Carla smiles at him, "Hermes saved us on the boat when we were sailing away. It was so bad ass! I never saw so much blood!" She seemed way too excited about it like she was fangirling.

"As the boat was floating away and you were disappearing from view, Hermes came up from the water, slipped onto the boat and used this big gun to blast the bad guys! There were pieces of them everywhere! Then we drove back to the dock and we watched it all unfold while trying to get back as quickly as possible. It was so chaotic!" Carla yells out. Hermes winks and she immediately turned red. There's definitely a story there but another time.

"O... kay. Nice to meet you. Thanks for saving my friends. Where is Daniel?"

He seemed shocked when I called him by his actual name. "Wow." He walked over to the window and chuckled to himself as he shook his head, "My boy. I knew he was in deep when the agency warned me he used his alternate code name. You know he is the only one who hides his darkness under another name. Zeus is his normal code name, but that night he brought out Hades after more than a decade. It was then we knew there was no going back for him. When he becomes Hades it's like a possession and he will leave with nothing less than utter carnage. And what you would see would give elite assassins like myself nightmares. Jimmy triggered him badly when he took you right in front of him. You girls are lucky you didn't see what he did to Jimmy or what was left of him. Even I have nightmares." He looks over at me. "Anyway, it all makes sense why he would want to request retirement. He deserves peace now."

I felt myself blush, but he still didn't answer me. "Where is he? Can I see him, please?" I felt the lump in my throat as I swallowed my pride.

"Not yet. I am working on getting you clearance from the agency. We have him in a secure wing of the hospital. He's...fighting hard. Stay positive. I am certain your presence will coax him to come back."

"How bad is it?"

Faster than an eye blink, I noticed his hesitation in answering me. Even a well-trained assassin is still a human being with emotions. He sighed heavily, "Jimmy shot him twice, once in the shoulder area and the other in his upper leg near the femoral artery. He flatlined twice due to the excessive blood loss, but they were able to revive him, stop the bleeding, and cauterize the wound, but he's been in a coma since then."

I couldn't help the sob that ripped through me as I felt a sharp pain in my heart. Milli pulls me to her, rocking me back and forth until I am quiet, in my thoughts, praying he'll make it. The physical pain I felt was nothing knowing that he died twice all alone.

I felt my bed dip and Hermes sat next to me, holding my hand. "Now, I'm not one for expressing emotion, doesn't fit the killer aesthetic, but I could tell from the moment he started talking to us about you that his career was over. He just wanted to live as a man."

"Us?"

Just then, another guy comes in; he's smaller in stature but still quite intimidating, and of course, impeccably dressed in a suit. Must be part of their dress code. "Meet Ares. He and I went with Zeus for that priority one assignment and…"

Ares stepped forward, "I knew immediately he was compromised because he was distracted by something or someone, rather. In all the years we worked together not once has he ever been that preoccupied before. After the job was done, we found out about your fight. The remorse he felt and the unknown at what to do. It was also then he brought up the idea of retirement…for you. You have to understand for us, that is a big deal. We have a better chance of dying on the job than to enjoy a life after this."

Hermes cringed and they could see my distress when hearing that, "Sorry, but it's the truth. I know he's looking forward to living a normal life with you. I also believe you can help with his recovery, but the agency is wrapping up all the legalities, including his final payment for Jimmy's kill.

Hermes stands up, "We're going to go visit him and tell him that you're awake. The moment you are cleared I will take you to him myself. Take care of yourself. You girls make sure she listens to the doctors."

"Okay." They answered in unison and then proceeded to tell me in more detail what happened while they were on their way to Cuba. It was more gruesome the second time, to say the least, but thank goodness for Hermes and Ares being assigned with Daniel. The outcome could have been so much worse.

I am thankful everyone was safe...

"Wait, where's Kayla?"

The entire room went silent and there was now an air of sadness.

"Oh, Emmy..." No other words had to be said. I now remember her lurching forward before her body was on top of mine and I passed out. I thought maybe she was knocked unconscious but judging by their faces, I was wrong.

"She...she didn't make it did she?" Carla shook her head with fresh tears in her eyes. "Jimmy shot her after she attacked him while trying to help you. She was dead before the ambulance made it."

I let my head fall as I silently wept for Kayla, not only her death but the trouble she went through. All she wanted was to be loved and cared for. It wasn't as crazy as it seemed; in a way, we were all looking for it, Kayla just fell for the wrong guy. The only good thing is she knew I wasn't upset with her for what she did.

"I shouldn't have beat her up! I'll never forgive myself; I was so angry! How could she do that to us? I thought we were sisters?!" Carla wailed as she chastised herself.

"She fell for the wrong man is all. I told her we would all be okay after she sought help. She knew you were angry, but she was going to fix it. You have to forgive yourself; it's not your fault. She wouldn't want you to feel this way. Let's sit here for a moment and mourn her. We will remember who she was as a sweet person and not her mistakes. Hating her won't bring her back but forgiving her will keep her memories alive within us.

And for a few moments, we remembered Kayla the way she was.

Colin/Daniel

Darkness, that's all that is around me, that, and the memories. I remember seeing the white light that everyone with near-death experiences always talks about. It came to me as a ball of concentrated white light. It radiated a soft light around me, feeling comforting, almost alluring, and tempting me to touch the orb in the center, but I heard a familiar voice.

Not yet, son. You have someone back there that loves you. It is not your time. Fight, fight to get back to her.

Mom.

With those words, the orb disappeared, and I was in my thoughts yet again. Does that mean Emmy was okay if I went back? The last memory was seeing her motionless on the ground before my injuries overwhelmed me. I imagined her voice whispering for me to come back, to not leave her here alone in this world, and to open my eyes.

I'm trying, princess.

Emmy

It had been two days since I last saw Hermes and still hadn't been clear to see Daniel. I was starting to feel hopeless, maybe they would never let me see him. It's because of me that he was here in the first place.

I missed him so much. Now, I realize calling him Colin felt wrong, especially when he looked me dead in the eye and told me that Daniel loved Ember.

Daniel loved me and I surely loved him, he was my protector, my provider, my everything. I felt so lost without him.

I wonder if there is a difference between Colin and Daniel, will his personality be different, will his mannerisms change? Or will he be the very same man whom I met on the site just with a different name?

I'm brought out my thoughts by my door opening. I thought it was the nurse taking my vitals for the millionth time, but it was Hermes.

I smiled from ear to ear in anticipation, "Can I see him?"

He returned the smile and for a killer, it was disturbing, borderline sadistic; he does not smile often.

"Yes, you have been cleared and added as his only visitor...as his wife. We finalized his portfolio and processed his retirement, deleting him from all databases as Colin Wentworth and creating a footprint of your lives together as husband and wife for the past nine months. It's the alternate option of going into witness protection, and me being the closest thing to a friend, I know he would not want to put you through that. So as of today, Colin Wentworth never existed.

So, Mrs. Daniel Denning, are you ready to see your husband?"

I smiled so hard my cheeks hurt. It sounded so natural, and I loved it. I didn't need some ceremony or a ring to make it official; I am his.

My mind wanted to process it all, but my legs wanted to run to him. Then I saw the nurse come in with a wheelchair, squashing part of my dream, of course.

"I can see you wanted to jump out the bed and run to him, but rules are rules, and you're still healing. I will push you there. Give me your hand." He gently lifts me from the bed and sets me in the chair. I wish I wasn't wearing this ugly gown or the sling, but it didn't matter; all I wanted was to lay eyes on him. As we passed the clipboard near my bed, I noticed my nametag said Denning and not Peters.

"We changed everything to reflect."

I guess if I get chosen for the kinesiology program, I have to tell them I got married while waiting.

That's if we stay here, what if we need to move?

Will I be able to find a program like this one?

Now I was concerned about my career and next steps. Not saying I wouldn't pick up and leave. I declared it to Daniel in that room, I would, but now...it was a lot to think about. I think Hermes noticed my furrowed brow.

"Thinking about the future?"

We go down a corridor that looks like it's going through construction. It's cordoned off with plastic. He couldn't be back here, could he? But we continue further in.

"Yeah, there's a program I applied for, I've been waiting to see if I got in, but if we have to move, I wonder if I can find something similar elsewhere."

"Kinesiology is quite a particular area of study."

"How did you..." He deadpans me. Of course, the "agency," whoever that is, obviously did a thorough background check on me.

"They do monitor the agents to make sure that whatever they are involved in doesn't compromise them and you, my dear, were his downfall."

We turned down yet another hallway. I wasn't even sure this was still part of the hospital. There were no visible markings to denote any medical care.

"You keep saying compromised. What exactly does that mean?"

"It means that Zeus became a liability when he allowed his feelings to override his cold and cunning execution skills. In short, when he fell in love, he became useless to us, but he gave us a couple of decades of his life, it's time for him to put himself first and not the agency. He deserves it. I'm going to tell you something he would kill me to find out I told you, but you are the only woman to tolerate this lifestyle. He never talked about a woman more than once, twice if I coerced him and by then, he said it was over. You flipped a switch in him, and I saw the human side to the cold-blooded killer. You're what he needs."

I didn't feel deserving of the niceties when I angrily walked out and gave up on us. Maybe it was I who didn't deserve him. I sniffle as we make another turn, but I see Ares standing at a door, so I knew we were here, wherever that was.

He stops me right before the door. Ares smiles, again, also a bit creepy, "Morning, Emmy. He's still unconscious but his vitals have been improving the last few days since we told him you were awake and would come to see him. Maybe you being near and talking to him can be the variable that brings him back."

I sigh long, deep, and hard, readying myself to see him. I try not to think negatively and push those thoughts way down deep, I needed to stay positive for him. "Okay, I'm ready." Ares pushes the door open as he steps in and holds it while Hermes rolls me inside. The room looked drastically different from the construction outside. It was beautifully decorated and almost didn't look like a hospital room, but the reality was that it was with all the machines, the beeps, clicks, and various medical noises.

He lay there, but he never looked more handsome even with his hair disheveled and out of place. His leg was exposed and heavily bandaged, you could see the wounds were still fresh and was still healing from the surgery. I think he also had a catheter being unconscious and all, but I will spare him that embarrassing tidbit of information. I just want him to wake up.

His shoulder also wrapped up from his elbow and around his chest to anchor it to prevent movement. Even the glimpse of his chest made me weak. He was sporting a black eye and some bruises on his hands, it's obvious he fought his way out, hopefully beating Jimmy to a pulp.

The good news was he was breathing on his own and didn't need a machine to assist him. I took his hand, kissed it gently, then stood up and placed my head on his chest to hear his heartbeat. He was warm to the touch and that gave me some hope as the tears rolled down and soaked his gown.

"Please...come back. Daniel, come back. I need you here with me." I squeezed his hand, so he knew that I was here, and I watched his chest rise and fall but no response. "I'm not giving up on you! You have to come back, we have so much to do together! Your princess needs her Daddy." I whispered the last part in his ear then kissed his cheek.

Still, nothing and I sat back in my chair, but I didn't let his hand go. The act of standing wore me out. I spent a few more minutes whispering things so that he could hear them in his subconscious. I brushed his hair back into the place. About ten minutes later, Hermes and Ares came in and a doctor followed in behind them.

"Emmy, this is Doctor Hill. He has been assigned to take care of Ze...Daniel."

"Hello, Mrs. Denning, I hope you are recovering as well. Mr. Denning has been improving daily. His injuries are healing on schedule, and we've been able to avoid any infections. It's now up to him when he wants to wake up, but we will continue to provide top-notch treatment until he is released.

"Thank you, Doctor, for all you've done." They gave me another five minutes before I had to go back and get my bandages replaced. It pained me to leave him. I stood once more and kissed his forehead, "Come back to me,

Daniel. Come back." And with that, I head back to my room, praying that he heard my plea.

Daniel

"Come back to me, Daniel. Come back."

Hearing her call, me by my real name made me feel invincible like I could take on the world! Her words seemed closer than before, like she was right next to me, but I was still in the voids of my mind, but I think I was slowly coming back. When I first recognized her voice, it had an echo like she was miles away, but that last plea was right next to me. I needed to get back to her; I just didn't know how.

Emmy

I was released from the hospital several days after I first visited Daniel. I made sure to see him twice a day with the help of the nurses. Hermes and Ares had assignments to complete since they were now down one teammate. On the last day, I told him I was going home, and I couldn't wait for when he would lie next to me. Then we could figure out what the rest of our lives would look like.

I hated being away from him, but I was more than ready to be home with two weeks under my belt in the hospital.

Milli told me they had the house professionally cleaned and rearranged the common areas, removing the old furniture and clearing out Kayla's belongings, except our group photo from her birthday celebration. They even cleaned up my room and put it back together from the chaos of my kidnapping.

It was so good to be in my bed, but also it felt empty, and he never once stepped foot in my room.

I asked Tawny to purchase a new laptop for me, I still needed it for the program. After setting it up and downloading all my programs, I found myself on Sweetsugar just to stare at his page. Noticing his last login was that fateful night I was taken right in front of him. I find myself reading the new comments from girls telling him how handsome he is and to contact them for a good time. I felt territorial.

Daddysbaby2001: Hey, Big daddy, you're so sexy! You want to be my sugar daddy?

Kittenwantstoplay: Isn't he sexy? He's also very taken, so keep it moving. First and LAST warning, thanks!

Another one:
Danielleneedsadaddy: I can be your princess. I'll send you nudes like a good girl. Just say the word.

Kittenwantstoplay: No, you can't, he already has his princess and that's me!

At that moment, I realized how much I missed him, and I cuddled up to my pillow to close my eyes and fantasize, remaining hopeful for better days ahead.

After being home another five days, we are slowly returning to a normal-like life, but we will never be the same. I'm slowly getting around the house, but I don't want to venture into the outside world. Today I was lounging out at the pool with my study materials. I have so much difficulty with the extensive torso area and the organs surrounding the muscle.

"Emmy! Emmy! It's here, the letter from the university program, open it, open it, open it! Tawny, Milli, it's here! Come quick!"

Before I could absorb the information, Carla was waving an envelope in front of my face. I grabbed it because the movement made me dizzy. I had to close my eyes and take a deep breath.

I look and indeed see the gold crescent logo for the program. I thought I had missed it while in the hospital, but the girls assured me they checked the mail and answered the house phone religiously.

"It's here, it's finally here and yet... I actually don't care if I got in or not." I lean back into the chair and toss the letter to the side.

"What? Are you freaking kidding me? You studied your ass off to get to this moment. You've been stalking that mailbox, your email, and every phone call and now you don't care? Look, I know you are worried about Colin..."

"Daniel."

"Sorry, I mean Daniel, but I know he would tell you to open it! Don't you want to share the news with him?"

"Yeah, you're right." I tear into the envelope and unfold the letter. "Dear Miss Peters, thank you for applying...blah blah blah...excellent package and work ethic...blah blah blah...congratulations you have been accepted into the fall program starting August 19th. OH MY GOD! I GOT IN! I GOT INNNN!!!!!" I screamed at the top of my lungs as they jumped up and down, each one hugging me separately, trying to avoid my injury because I was still sporting a sling.

The phone rang in the house and Carla went in to answer as we squealed and danced to the news of the century. I was on my way to fulfilling my lifelong dream!

Carla opens the patio door, "Umm, just an idea...we should celebrate! Tawny and I will go get stuff to make dinner. Come on, Tawny." She follows her and Carla whispers something in her ear and she gasps before clapping her hands as they leave. I looked at Milli, who was looking at her phone.

"I wonder what that was all about?"

Milli is smiling from ear to ear, but then she looks at me and shrugs. "Why don't you go get ready? Carla texted and said we're all going to dress up in celebration. Let me know if you need help. I'm going to go set up the dining room." I concede and head to my room to prepare a bath. I use a lavender and honey-scented bath bomb and I sink into the tub. It is hard to maneuver the washing on one side and they always offer to help me, but they didn't know that I take the sling off and use the arm to gently wash the other side. My range of motion has improved, so the sling was more of an option and not a necessity, but I won't willingly convey that info to my doctor. I carefully climb out of the bath 20 minutes later and smooth on a body butter in the same lavender honey scent. I thought it was the one scent I wanted Daniel to associate me with.

Then my heart sank. I can't wait to visit him tomorrow and relay the good news! They said Daniel was getting better, so I hope that tomorrow his dreamy eyes meet mine.

I wrap a body towel around as I walk from the bathroom into my walk-in closet, noting it was almost 8 o'clock, the perfect time for dinner and celebratory cocktails. Maybe there'd be cake!

We had a beautiful outside bar by the pool, so maybe we could have some music, turn on the pool lights, and have our own mini-club setting.

My actual clubbing days are over, not only because I would put a bullet in Dominic's head the first chance I get, but there's no need to seek what I have, and I have Daniel. My husband. I love randomly saying that, or our names together. Ember Denning, Emmy and Daniel Denning, the Denning's.

I couldn't help but laugh happily at how silly it was.

I contemplate my outfit and go for a simple spaghetti strap little black dress with a double ruffle accent bottom. I paired it with chunky silver heels that weren't nosebleed, I still had to contend with my balance with this brace. I toss the towels in the hamper, and I go back into the bathroom.

"Emmy, are you almost done?" I hear Carla yell.

"Yeah, give me three minutes and I'll be right out!" I kept my makeup simple with mascara and wine-colored lipstick. We weren't actually going anywhere but after hospital gowns and loungewear for the longest, it's nice to get dolled up a bit. Maybe I'll send him a picture to his inbox. I look over myself in the mirror but then I hear a knock on the door.

They are so impatient!

I roll my eyes, "Good grief, I said I'm coming!"

I hope I wasn't overdressed, but they did say to get dolled up. This would make for amazing photos even with the sling, at least it was black and matched. I managed to slip it back on after finishing up.

Then they knocked once more, "Okay, I said I was coming! You guys act like we're going some..." As I opened the door my words died right there on my lips.

Was I dreaming? I had to be because there Daniel was right in front of me. He was leaning against a cane, but he was impeccably dressed in a dark royal blue suit and crisp white button-up that had the top two buttons undone, giving me a peek of his chest. My heart was beating so hard I could hear the blood rushing.

I could tell it wasn't one of his usual assassin suits, those were usually black or gray. No, this attire was bought for a special occasion and that was him stepping foot into my home. I was distracted by that smile that always made me swoon. He eyed me hungrily as he raked up and down my figure, then he bit his lip. "Well, hello, little one, did you miss me?"

I threw myself on him wrapping my good arm around him but noticing him trying to balance us after I slammed into him. It also didn't help with my injured arm as well, it hurt like hell, but I didn't care! I rocked us as I felt the laughter rumble in his chest, if we kept going, I am sure we'd end up on the floor more injured than we are now. I didn't want to let go, but I also wanted to see his handsome face.

"Are you really here?! In my house? When did you wake up, how did you get here? Oh, I have so many questions!" I laugh as his strong hand caresses my cheek, wiping away the tears of joy. All I could do was smile and bask in the moment until I hear squealing noises behind us, and I see my girls smiling from ear to ear. I'm almost certain they set me up.

Daniel

Not to taint the touching moment when she opened her bedroom door, but I saw her in that amazing little black dress and now I am dealing with a raging erection. I mean it is screaming to feel her climax all over me and hear her call me Daniel. To hear her scream it as I thread my fingers through her hair, tightening my grip as I slam deliciously into her, brushing against her clit until she's convulsing uncontrollably around my dick, maybe my princess is a squirter.

My explicit fantasy made it worse, but I will it down because I want to start this romantic night I had planned with the help of her friends once I knew I was being released.

"Let's head to the dining room; Carla made dinner for us." She looked shocked as she looked back at them. "Are you guys leaving?" They all nod their heads and wave before exiting the house. I sent them to dinner and a movie. You know, to one of those movie theaters you can order food and drinks while you wait for the movie to start.

I focused back to see her with a raised brow, "You set this up with the girls, didn't you?!" She exclaimed.

I had her walk in front of me to lead me to the dining room. It was a pretty big place for the area they were in. I also got to watch her in that dangerously short dress that made her legs look a mile long and her ass sat high and was begging for a good licking from me. I couldn't use my free hand because I should be using a sling, but I refused. I had to negotiate for the cane. They wanted me on crutches, but I refused to see my kitten looking all banged up, bringing up the awful memories of that night that my bruises didn't already convey.

We made it slowly to the dining room where she stopped at the threshold. She gasped when she saw the surroundings, "Oh, Daniel, it's so romantic."

There it was my name from her lips. Something so simple yet it had so much power and held some very lustful undertones. Oh, how the roles reversed, now daddy was the needy one.

I had Hermes help me with some items I needed to make this scene a reality. The whole squad came by to visit before my release from the hospital and immediate retirement status. Hermes was promoted to the top position, and it made sense even though he was a crazy bastard and I'm sure my replacement will be someone much younger and more agile than this old man. I was fortunate to be granted a chance to say goodbye. I even got a call from Socrates who wished me all the best and that he told me so. I couldn't argue.

I had Hermes go purchase two dozen red roses and rose petals that were placed all over the table. The girls lit some candles and fixed our plates. I see the champagne bottle was already open with the cork placed on top. I limp ahead to pull her chair out. She sits and crosses her legs making her dress even shorter. I heard myself groan and when I looked down at her, she smiled and winked.

I couldn't take it anymore, I took that moment to grab her by the back of her neck, forcing her to look directly at me. She gasped at the sudden and aggressive movement.

My dominance wants control. I gaze at her full lips staring back at me, begging to be kissed, but I need her permission.

"Can daddy kiss you?"

Her beautiful gaze went wide, glazing over in anticipation. Her breath staggered, the excitement almost too much.

"Pl-please."

I leaned down to kiss those lips, not at a time where we were in a precarious situation or facing death, just a normal kiss between a man and a woman. I found myself losing all sense of control, she tasted sweet like honey and smelled like it too with hints of lavender. Her hands came up to find themselves tangling in my hair. I pull away with my dominance demanding to take her.

Patience, tiger.

"Okay, we better stop, or we won't make it through dinner."

"Oh, ok." She blushed while bowing submissively but I lifted her chin, "I'm so happy to have you in front of me looking stunningly gorgeous." She giggled in response. Her blush deepened a bit more, she's so cute.

Knowing she's old enough to drink, I pour her a glass of champagne. I sit across the table from her and pour my glass, watching her little nuances, watching her watch me. I can tell that she's anxious as she sips her champagne to avoid blatantly staring at me and letting her mind wander.

There was a heavy silence, filled with anxiety, passion, and most of all lust. If I had two good arms, I'd rip her dress off and take her on the dining room table, but I suppress the thought but add it on my *"do to her list"*.

"I suppose I should tell you what happened. Well, I woke up two days ago, Hermes was going to let you know but I didn't want you coming back up there, I wanted to surprise you by showing up at your door. That's why I called and told the girls I wanted to put together an intimate dinner with the two of us. Then a little birdie told me some amazing news. Congratulations, pussy cat. You worked so hard; you deserve it."

She seemed surprised that I even knew but the girls couldn't wait to tell me. "Thank you, but...what happens to you? Where will you go? Wherever it is I want to go with you! I don't need much; I can be packed and ready to go by morning. I just...I can't be away from you again." She looked so afraid that I might disappear right in front of her.

The fact that she's ready to pick up and move anywhere with me is mind-blowing. It also confirms the decisions I already set into motion.

I swirl my champagne then lift the glass, "Cheers to my kitten on her acceptance into the university's kinesiology program, your lifelong dream starts now and because of that, you won't need to move very far. I found a beautiful skyrise condo about four blocks from here and near the campus so you can walk there and back. And don't worry about the girls, I found a three-bedroom condo in the building next to us, you'll all be together. I suppose I'll spend that time adjusting to retired life, I don't know, maybe I'll take up golf or fly fishing."

Neither of those sounds very interesting, I felt old saying that.

She jumped up and before I knew it, she was on my lap kissing me profusely. I ignored the sharp pain but couldn't help but grunt. She notices and shifts to the other leg. "Oh, I'm sorry!" She kisses me sweetly before running her hand over my face, across my jawline, "That sounds like something an old guy would say. I'm sure you'll find something to pass the time. It doesn't have to be anything you see on those senior community commercials, you're still in your prime. Maybe try surfing or beach volleyball. Thank you, so much, thank you! Can you really afford all that?"

She's adorable.

"I paid the rent for their condo for a year so they can save up for when the next year starts. They are responsible for utilities, but our place is paid in full. And I still have several million left."

She sputtered, "Sev- sev-several million?!" She tried to continue but nothing came out but a high-pitched squeak, so I explained, "Twenty plus years and no big expenses like a car or house I was able to save 95% of what I earned for each job. I think the most luxurious things I splurged on were maybe some of my hotel rooms and my designer suits."

She licked her lips while eyeing me. "Mmm, when I did see you in a suit it always made me so...so..." She trails off but I already know what she was going to say. It made her wet at the sight of me, I always made it a point to pull up my sleeves while talking to her, I knew the message it expressed. I could see the desire in her eyes and feel her devouring me through the screen.

Right now, she's trying to get through the night. We're both part of the same passionate flame, trying to do things the way a normal couple would. The awkwardness of the first date, getting to know each other and then becoming comfortable enough to be intimate.

Like normal people...

And I started to really think about it. We met online; all interactions prior had been online except the fight. She obviously had a daddy kink and liked to roleplay as a kitten. I wanted to learn to be more dominant. She was learning to be my submissive. We spent a lot of time talking about stuff we read on Naughtyfet, sending each other articles that helped us understand our roles. Why should we conform to society's norms we were already breaking?

I patted her ass to signal her to stand. A gasp escaped her lips, she was hanging on by a thread.

Emmy

So much has happened including both of us ending up in the hospital. Knowing he almost died twice while I was in my hospital bed healing terrified me even with him looking at me now. He could have died while I was unconscious, but instead, he fought back from the brink of death to show up at my door, looking as handsome as ever.

I was already fantasizing about the ways he would take me, including right here on this table. If I was wearing underwear they'd be soaked by now. I squeeze my thighs as he stares down at me making me squirm even further. He signals me to stand then he pulls me against him. I can feel his heartbeat twice, in his chest and against my upper thigh. He was absolutely throbbing hard.

My breathing hitches. I can't catch my breath; it feels like I ran a marathon.

He's struggling with his control as well, screw it, I wasn't even that hungry, anyway. I lick my lips and lean up towards him.

"I need you."

A low, guttural, aggressive growl slips his lips, and I was covered in goosebumps, "Bedroom, now." I sauntered past and finally felt him as his hand smacked my ass hard, the sound reverberated through the house. I wonder if he could tell I wasn't wearing any underwear.

This was not how I expected our first rendezvous to go but we have gone through way too much since I stupidly walked away, and I won't spend another minute not under the man who makes my heart flutter. I look back to see him eagerly but slowly make his way behind me.

I leaned against my bedroom door frame then, when he was closer, I stepped into my room a bit more, faced away, and slipped off my dress letting it drop to the floor.

Luckily, I could unzip it with one hand. I slip the sling off and carefully let my hand fall to the side only feeling a bit of strain on my arm. I'm startled when I suddenly feel his breath brush my neck.

Then he tsks while his fingertips run up my arm, the feeling is electric. "I don't think you're supposed to take off your sling. In fact, I'm quite sure. What a naughty little pussy cat, defying doctor's orders and on top of that, you aren't wearing underwear. I think that deserves punishment but first, daddy wants to meet his kitten, tail, and all. Go."

As quickly as I could, I went into my drawer and pulled out my black lace ears and fingerless lace gloves. I had to reach further back for my black and white tail which took a bit of effort to insert. I had only tried it twice, it wasn't painful, just uncomfortable, and snug from lack of use. Luckily, it was beginner-sized, the smallest one I could get. Daddy thinks I don't like the plug, but once I am used to it, it feels amazing.

After completing the look, I climb on the bed, lie on my back, and purr. I looked over to see him palming himself before he sat down on the other side of the bed. I sit up on my hands and knees waiting for the next command.

"Across my lap." I keep my back arch deep to accentuate the curve of my ass before slowly sliding across his lap and obvious erection. He rubbed and squeezed my ass, sending chills up my spine, causing me to purr in anticipation.

"Oh, pussy cat, you sound so needy…"

I'm not the only one. I think it got harder during the time I slid across his lap.

Wow.

smack I jumped and nearly fell to the floor, but his strong hand caught me and put me back in position.

"That's for not listening to me at the hotel," **smack** "and that's for yelling and calling me by my first name." **smack** "for being a tease and not wearing underwear and," **smack** "this is for not saying thank you after every spank. Who's daddy's good girl?"

This was my first official punishment as his sub and I think with him equally learning his role he took it easy on me with just the spanking, I'm sure there will be other options for punishment later. Although my ass was on fire, I beamed when he asked me who was daddy's good girl.

"I'm sorry. Thank you, daddy. I'm daddy's good girl." He rubs my tingling cheeks, lost in the feeling of my skin. He was practically salivating then he chuckles, it's low and dominant. I'm caught off guard when he tugs at my tail. That tug made the pulsing even stronger; he was pulling me closer to the edge especially as he placed kisses all over the curve of my ass.

"Position one."

I scramble quickly to sit back on my legs, spine rigid with my palms up, staring straight ahead. He doesn't know it, but I would practice in front of the mirror to make sure my legs or arms wouldn't shake after an extended period of time. I wanted to impress him with my ability to be perfectly still. I don't look to see his approval, but in my mind, I know he is and I'm happy.

He stands, pulling off his jacket. Something he always does when he's on the phone with me right before he pulls up his sleeves. I can't describe how mouthwatering that gesture is to me, it just is, but it's a thousand times sexier in person.

He does me a favor by standing in my view so I can still watch my favorite part of our talks. I wanted to lick my lips at the sight of him, but I keep my position obediently.

He slowly reached for the cuff of his sleeve. "You have no idea how much I've fantasized about our first night together. I could have never guessed everything that happened in between…"

One cufflink undone.

"How did such a stunning and intelligent beauty cross my path? And right before I was about to delete my profile."

The other cufflink.

"I felt so unworthy of a girl like you. Colin was Daniel's protector, but I didn't know how to bring Daniel back. Colin was cold, devious, stealthy, but emotionless. Everything needed to be a killer."

Roll sleeves up.

"I didn't want to present that to you once I got to know you. I knew you were special."

He kneels on the ground, and he's face to face with me. I almost jump when his warm hands slide from my knees up to my thighs. I try to keep my position and my composure knowing he's inches away from my throbbing pussy and he's constantly squeezing. I am on a hair-trigger and teetering towards orgasm. I think he knows how badly this is affecting me, so he slides his thumb inward trying to get me to react, but I stay perfectly still.

"What a good girl... so obedient. You can release from position one." He moves and now he's slightly behind me, then he growled in my ear.

I can't explain what happened next but having him this close caused my senses to overload. I groaned and shuddered violently then grunted. I was leaning almost enough to fall forward before I regained my senses and sat back.

He raised his brow and stood up while observing me.

I could only bite my lip, hard.

"Kitten... did you just cum?"

We're still learning this sub/dom situation, but I knew enough, and I know I wasn't supposed to cum without his permission. I lowered my head in shame.

Now I was certain I was going to get punished. He could deny me orgasm or tell me I'm not allowed to touch Daddy! The possibilities were endless! I was now shaking in fear instead of pleasure and I felt the tears well up.

"I'm sorry daddy, I didn't mean to." I look up and he wipes my tears away.

"No, no, no... it's ok, I'm not mad. In fact, that was the single sexiest thing I've ever seen. Your reaction of me merely touching you, so reactive to Daddy's touch... fuck, baby..."

"I've been so anxious and eager to feel Daddy. So many wet dreams and fantasies and now you're here. I want you to touch me, I need you to touch me. My body is yours... to do whatever you want; I want to make you happy."

Daniel

She wanted to make me happy. No sweeter words have been spoken but it was me who was here to please her.

I leaned in, kissing her slowly and methodically to rile her up again, obviously, it won't take much. This time I would be the direct cause of her next leg shaking orgasm. As our tongues wrestle she allows me to dominate. I take that opportunity of distraction to slide my fingers across her sensitive and slick pussy. She gasped in my mouth then I pulled back and slowly brought my fingers to my lips.

Watching her watch me taste her was the sweetest moment as she finally graced my tongue. I smirk watching her pant. Her taste was addictive and I want more.

"Take it off." She reaches behind and unclips her bra. I stare at her beautiful breasts as she scoots back pulling me up on the bed by my open shirt. I like where she's going with this. Now we're at a standstill.

We're so close I can feel her breath on me as we both sit on our knees. I reach over and pull her ears off and toss the headband towards the dresser, not knowing if I hit it or not. I was not going to take my gaze off her. She slips her fingers out her gloves and tosses them in the same direction.

There was one final piece, who would take it out? She reached back and with a bit of effort pulled her tail out, she moaned out her relief. She tosses it with the same carelessness as earlier. With the heaviness of the small metal plug, I heard it hit the dresser before it clanged on the floor.

She holds her hand up while gazing at me and I follow her movement then press my hand to hers, she wraps her fingers around mine and I do the same. She repeats with the other hand. I catch her breasts swaying as I scoot even closer. I look up from them and see her eyes lit by the flames of lust.

It was electric between us, the days, weeks, months of built-up anticipation. None of the lies mattered, the argument, the time apart, it all meant nothing when we both ended up in the hospital. I could have lost my princess; I had no idea how severe her injuries were. Thank goodness it was minor compared to my injuries, but I'd gladly take the brunt of the pain for her. And now, I'm staring at the one person who loves me.

She loves me. What more could I ever need?

"Daddy?" She breaks me out of my thoughts.

"Yes, little one?" I brush a lock of hair behind her ear. "My arm hurts." She dropped her hand and I laughed. I had a bit of pain in my shoulder, but my leg was okay. It was a sign that we both needed a break.

"Lay down." I help her lie flat and prop her arm up with a pillow. "But...I want to touch you, too. I've been waiting for so long." She whines.

I hover over her, "No whining...you'll have plenty of time. I want to finally claim every inch of my princess from head to toe." I smile and tickle her which makes her laugh.

I can put weight on my injured arm, but I shift most of it to the other. I don't want to end up on Sex Sent Me to the ER. It is completely possible, especially at my age.

I maneuver myself down so I can kiss her forehead, a symbol of everlasting love, then her cute little nose, and her pouty awaiting lips. I stole a few more there before making my way lower, from her chin down her delicate neckline and the hollow spot between her breasts causing her to giggle. It sounded more like a combination of a sigh, giggle, and moan. Either way, it provoked me to go further.

"More..." She arches her back as her hand pulls my hair. She bucked a little when I licked and swirled around each nipple, sealing the deal with a kiss. She pulled my hair even tighter, as I noted another sweet spot.

Her skin was warm as I kissed down her abdomen and licked her belly button. She looked down, wondering what the hell I was doing. I was curious to see her reaction...she was not amused or turned on...moving on.

I veered left to nibble on her hip and her grip tightened again as she squirmed. "Mmm..." I kiss my way over to the right hip before placing an innocent kiss right below her belly button, looking up at her. I slid back so I lay flat, sitting on my elbows and forearms, which helped to distribute my weight.

I stay silent on purpose, to build anticipation and torture her a bit. She's pouting at the lack of physical touch and because I'm sure she can feel my breath on her pussy. I intentionally breathe in deep to exhale against her. She is completely and utterly soaked more than before, and I can smell her sweet arousal.

"What do you want? Tell me." I place a chaste kiss on her lower lips, and she arches her back. "That daddy, more, please! I...." Then she stopped and I saw her mood change.

"I need to say something."

Like, right now?!

I can feel my erection thumping against the bed but whatever she has to say seems very important, important enough to interrupt me, so I nod reluctantly.

"I wasn't a good girl. I was stubborn and hot-tempered, willing to throw it all away. Hermes and Ares showered me with such praise about how I changed you for the better and that I made you happy, but I didn't deserve it. I was a brat. I walked away... I'm sorry, for being so immature, for trying to make you jealous when I took that picture with Dom, for not having you here after Jimmy felt me up. I wanted you here so badly! I was wrong, can you forgive me?"

A whole speech while I sat there, eye level with her pussy. There's only one way to answer...

I bury myself in her, catching her off guard as her ticklish squeals turn into moans. I tighten my hold as much as my injury can tolerate because she's trying to run from me.

Nowhere to go, kitten.

"Da... daddy, yes!"

Hmm, that's not it.

I needed to hear it again, but in the throes of passion, not when she was screaming at me or whimpering in fear. I needed to hear it lustfully. "Call me Daniel. It drives me wild."

"Daniel, please." She begs and I was straining to keep control. I focus on sending her into orgasmic bliss. Licking, swirling and lightly nibbling. She scratches up my arm as her moans signal, she was so close. Then I pulled back, and she looked devastated.

Emmy

*W*hat the hell?! I was so close! I knew he was going
to punish me!

I felt the tears pooling, "Am I being punished?"

"What? No, I want to feel you orgasm around my
dick."

Oh. He scoots forward bumping his dick against my
clit until it rests on top. I'm not going to make it with all
this teasing! He kisses me so sweetly and I taste myself on
him.

He chuckles, "Truth be told, I'm such a pushover as a
daddy. I don't think I could ever really punish my
princess."

I scoff, "Well, you're going to have to learn. Right
now, we're just playing on my kink and pet play. You said
you want me as your submissive and that takes discipline
from time to time. We both have to learn; besides I know
it's out of love and lust, mainly lust. I love when my
daddy dom has total control over me in the bedroom,
telling me what to do." I stare for a moment, then I wink.
I thought I had the upper hand until he slid into me
without batting an eye and I jumped, squeezing my walls
against him.

"Holy fucking shit. Easy. Don't do that or I'm going to
explode."

He's trying to control his breathing while feeling the
mutual pulsing between us. I never experienced
something like this before. Every inch caused me to
squeeze in response.

"I can't! You feel...so good...but..."

I remember something I said in one of our sex sessions. I sit up on my elbows and tilt my head. He looked confused. "I need you on your back. Arm on the pillow, too." Much like how he had me positioned.

He raised his brow, "Are you asking me or telling me?"

"Please, daddy." He rolled on his good arm to lie flat on his back. I sat up on my knees leaning

against him. I traced his chest down to his rock-hard erection, he inhaled sharply as I continued down his left leg and back up his right. On the return trip, he grabs my wrist, "I'm only so strong."

"Sorry. Do you remember the night you made me cum so hard I was shaking and then you followed right after me? Remember I told you how..." I slip my leg over so that I'm straddling him, and I sit directly on him. "I wanted your hand wrapped around my throat while I rode you within an inch of your life?" His eyes widen as I sit up, line him up, and slide down slowly.

"Ohhhh my...shit!" He groans out. I lean forward just brushing against his lips. "I'm ready...after daddy says what I need to hear. Please."

I proceed to rock slowly, up and down, back and forth. I can see he's holding on by a thread of a thread but honestly, so am I. Just when I thought I had him in my grip he growls before he smirks and I'm even wetter causing me to speed up. Then his hand shot up and latched onto my throat.

"Is that what you want? Hmm? You want daddy to tell you to use him, use his rock-hard throbbing dick until you cum all over it. Let me wrap my hand around your neck as you ride me until your legs shake, your pussy aches and you make daddy all yours? Is that it?"

Fuck! That's exactly it, I am furiously rocking against him, the friction making me sensitive all over. I don't think I can form a cogent point until I'm shaking all over him.

I nod furiously, repeating "there!" as his good hand helps slam me down and push me back and forth. Both motions felt so good, but I was searching for that magical combination and then...his hand went from my hip back to squeezing my throat just enough.

"OH...Daniel!"

Then I open my eyes as I'm laying against his chest breathing hard. He brushes my hair away from my face.

"Welcome back." He kissed my forehead, and I placed my hand on his chest, resting my cheek on it. "What happened?"

"You came and then passed out. Only for a few seconds. It was the most incredible feeling ever, enough to send me overboard."

He pulls the blanket up with one hand, covering me up to my neck.

"We should probably shower."

"Let's just bask in it for a few minutes. I've waited too long to have you in my arms."

He kisses me on the forehead, and I realize he's right. We lay in comfortable silence for a while.

I don't know how long I was asleep, but I sat up to see he was still sleeping. He was gorgeous and I couldn't help but touch his lips which immediately turned into a smile then he kissed me quickly.

"I don't know about you, but I'm hungry now."

"Yeah, I bet the girls are probably back so we should be quiet." I slowly and carefully dismount to search for my robe. He puts on his boxers and his button-up and I arch my brow.

"Do you really want them to see me shirtless?"

Fair enough. I reach back for him, and he places his hand in mine but not before smacking my ass, hard. I felt the knot forming again. I started walking but he stopped me, "Princess, I need you to wear your brace. No argument."

He holds up the sling and I let him slip it over and I place my arm in it.

"Satisfied?" I state sarcastically.

"For now. Regarding the sling, yes, I want you to heal properly."

"Well, what about you, shouldn't you be using your cane?"

"I'm fine, this isn't about me. Now come on, I'm starving and I'm planning on eating you for dessert." He winks and the knot tightens. I find the strength to walk forward, out the door, and towards the kitchen.

I can hear chatter and hopefully, they didn't hear me scream out his name. I see them huddle around a carton of ice cream. Ice cream is food, right?

We are met with great big smiles. "So good to see the mister and missus again, we thought we would have to leave food by the door for the next week or so." They all laugh while continuing to indulge in the decadence before them.

He wraps his arms around me, "That is still a possibility."

Carla points towards the fridge, "We put the food away. We saw the untouched plates and we knew you'd be back for it...later." She winks and Daniel releases me to head straight for the fridge. He fixes a plate, loads it down with food then sticks it in the microwave.

I join the girls on the same side of the island and am handed a spoon for the turtle pecan ice cream. He takes the spoon and tsks, "Not yet, little one, have some dinner first then you can have ice cream." He kisses my forehead and I smile.

I can see they want to ask a million questions. Daniel sits down and I sit next to him. He gives me a quick peck while spinning the fork in the pasta.

I look around the stove and microwave, "Hey, where's mine?" I poke my lip out, did he really only make himself something to eat?

Then he brings the pasta laden fork to my lips. "I'll always take care of you first. This is enough for us both. Honestly, because of my job, I don't eat a lot of processed foods."

That's why he has the body of a 25-year-old gym rat. Maybe he should be my new fitness instructor with all his free time.

He takes a bigger forkful and shoves it in his mouth.

It's silent, too silent, even for them. Then I remember, "Oh! Tell them about your plan."

They look at him as he feeds me another forkful and I feed him the ice cream. "That is super sweet! Do you guys eat this regularly?" We all nod our heads as he shakes his. Well, more for us.

"Wow. Anyway, I told Emmy I didn't think it was safe to live here after the incident. So, she and I will be moving into a high-rise condo a few blocks away..."

I watched their faces fall, they all set their spoons down somberly. "Oh, that's nice. I'm happy for you guys, but I'm going to miss you, Emmy!" They all surround me in a warm hug. When we break apart I smile, "He wasn't done yet, tell them."

I noticed half the plate was now gone, that man could eat, in both ways. I try not to think about him telling me I would be his dessert later.

"Right, well I understand that this isn't just a friendship but a sisterhood and so I rented a condo in the adjacent building so while you may not be roommates, you'll be neighbors."

"WHAT?!" They all scream in unison and proceed to attack Daniel with hugs. "Thank you, thank you, thank you! Oh my gosh, you are the best! Emmy is such a lucky girl! We'll never be able to repay you for keeping us together!"

"It's no problem, I paid the rent for a year so you guys can come up with a plan to sustain afterward but you are responsible for utilities." They all squeal again and I enjoy the ice cream as they enjoy the good news.

"When do we move in?"

"I figure in two weeks since we're in the middle of the month. If you can find a local mover we can set it all up at the same time. In the meantime..." I feel him slide my chair his way to wrap his arms around me and kiss my shoulder. "I want to spend more time with my wife."

I blush but don't say anything as they swoon.

"Well, thank you for dinner and a movie, the condo, and being what our girl needs. We're going to bed. Breakfast is at 9 am! Night!"

"Night." We both say, then his hand lands on my upper thigh causing me to hiccup. I see that the plate is nearly gone. "It was delicious, but I'll definitely need to start my gym routine back up before I get a dad bod."

"There's nothing wrong with a dad bod and you should be able to enjoy your retirement. Relax and unwind." I turn and massage his neck and shoulders and feel him melt underneath my touch.

"How about... I treat my husband to a full-body massage. I'll be careful around your injuries."

He growled, "You bet your sweet ass. Oh, and don't think I forgot about you being my special dessert later. If I want to satisfy my sweet tooth I'll gladly do so by devouring you."

He takes the plate to the sink, washes it before drying, and putting it away. I put the ice cream in the freezer and followed him back to my room.

I gave him a five-star massage like promised and he gave me three additional orgasms that night.

Daniel

I was up at 7 am because I'm still a creature of terrible habit. I sit there and find myself brushing my fingertips against her smooth skin and watching her react while still asleep.

"Mmm." She moans before she snuggles into me further.

Don't rile me up, pussy cat.

I take deep breaths to calm my erection down, though I could go for a morning wake-up.

I didn't even realize she was awake as I was deep in my thoughts until I felt her hand on my dick and it caused me and it to jump.

"Whoa! Good morning to you, too, kitten. How'd you sleep?"

She yawned and stretched causing the blanket to sink down and reveal her perky breasts. How I wanted to devour them, but I had something I wanted us to do together first.

"Do you have your laptop around?"

She sits up and reaches over me to her nightstand to grab it and torture me by slowly rubbing against me before lying down on her side. She opened it up and there was my profile on her screen. I looked at her and she shrugged nonchalantly, "When I got released from the hospital I missed you so I was looking at your pictures. Also, I may have threatened a few girls to back off."

I read her response to a couple of the girls under my pictures. She was a combination of sweet and vicious, I loved it.

"It's ok, I would do the same." I log her off and log myself in. I have 78 messages, 246 likes, and 57 friend requests. I watch her watch me as I go to the settings and delete my account. It prompts me if I am sure and I look over to the radiant beauty who has my heart and smile before I kiss her deeply, "I love you, Ember."

She mirrored my action by logging back in. She had so many notifications it only showed a 99 followed by a plus sign. I'm not surprised, she's got beauty and most importantly brains. She had a dream she was pursuing and I am glad I get to watch her achieve her dreams. She hit enter to confirm the deletion of her page then she moved the laptop and straddled me, "And I love you, Daniel."

Words never sounded sweeter.

THE END

Assassinated by Love

About The Series

Thank you for reading book #1 of the
Lies & Production
Catfish Series

Stay tuned for:

Kissed by Death
Deadly Looks

And many more!
Follow us on
FB: <u>A Lies and Secrets Production | Facebook</u>
IG: <u>***A Lies & Secrets Prodution***</u>
<u>(@aliesandsecretsprod) • Instagram photos and videos</u>
For the latest and greatest!

S. Courtney Catalog

The Bound Series:
Fated mates, Paranormal Romance
Bound to You (#1)
Bound by Destiny (#2)
Unapologetically Nessa (#3)
Dark Fate: A Christian Tale (#4)*
Blood Bound (#5)*

 # indicates release order
*coming soon

Other Releases
The Black Aces MC (MC Romance)
The Sandman (Paranormal Romance)
The Merciless Few Anthology: Wrecked (MC
Romance)

Assassinated by Love

About The Author

S Courtney is new to the published writing community but has been a lifelong writer and began creatively writing in junior high.

She is the author of the paranormal romance, the Bound Series, which includes Bound to You, Bound by Destiny, and Unapologetically Nessa which are available on paperback and kindle.

She is also the author of her contemporary romance, the Black Aces MC, a motorcycle club romance and the Sandman, a dark, slow burn paranormal romance.

Assassinated by Love

Social Links

Stay in Touch!

Email: authormskeiya@yahoo.com

FB Author Page: www.facebook.com/authormskeiya

Instagram:
www.intstagram.com/author_mskeiya

Bookbub:
www.bookbub.com/profile/s-courtney

Website (sign up for my newsletter!):
https://www.scourtneybooks.com/
LinkTree: https://linktr.ee/mskeiya

Assassinated by Love